TO THE BRINK OF MADNESS

Jean M. Warren

Co-Author: Donna J. Warren

TO THE BRINK OF MADNESS is a product of nonfiction. Names, places, characters, and incidents are a product of the author's imagtion or use fictitiously. Any resemblance to any persons, either living or deceased, events, or places is only coincidental.

TO THE BRINK OF MADNESS

Jean M. Warren

Co-Author: Donna J. Warren

I dedicate this book to Miss Alexis

Her everlasting love and kindness to me in Boarding School saved my life

ACKNOWLEDGEMENT

Today, child abuse is becoming more and more controversial. It has finally submerged upstream and into the open. Awareness of the actual existence in recent years has generated a powerful drive toward the correction of abuse and due to this energetic force I was inspired to write my book.

My story attributes to a horrid three year phase of my life spent in a boarding school. I unfold a truth of the intolerable torment and physical abuse I yielded in addition to an unforgettable love I lost.

In between these pages, is realized that abuse stemmed from the indifferent attitudes of adults and was rapidly exemplified by the young. Therefore, I point out to a vast audience that abusiveness can become a corrupt practice in any aspect and carried out mercilessly if not simmered or corrected.

The consequences an abused child sustains can be a traumatic experience. Subsequently, I suffered mental havoc. Physically my wounds have healed, but mentally my thoughts remain steadfast whereas I cope with uncertainties and I renounce love for fear of losing. I feel it has no business in my life and I can't seem to rationalize reality for my intense fear smothers all valuable intent.

MOMMIES PHANTOM FACE

Oh dainty little orphaned child

You're frenzied and beguiled

Daddy is unknown and Mommies passed on

And, you wish that you were gone

You yearn for her arms that once cradled you

And, for her sweet affection that made you coo

Your dreams are haunted by her "Phantom Face."

Of which you hold fast, in a loving embrace

Awakened from slumber, you shed tears of sorrow

Aware that her "Phantom Face" will be gone all tomorrows

You shade the reality that Mommies in heaven

And, it's created mixed emotions, all at the age of seven

CHAPTER 1

From the age of four, Gina recalls being shuttled to different foster homes. She didn't know why, except she remembers overhearing her foster parents chatter that her real parents had met with a fatal mishap when she was an infant and, soon after, was placed in an orphanage.

She never doubted the inevitable, but was always curious how they had met their death; and did she have brothers and sisters? Whenever she dared ask questions, they were dismissed; no one would give her a straight answer. All she recollects them talking about, was having made it through the "Great Depression" and getting back on their feet; and all Gina wanted was to be like other kids and boast about her own mommy and daddy, but knew it was senseless to dream of such grandeur. Despite all obstacles, she was flourishing reasonably content and was a happy-go-lucky child.

When Gina had reached the tender age of seven, Miss Jacobs, her social worker had other plans for her. It was cold, but sunny that first day of January when Miss Jacobs arrived at the foster home where Gina dwelt. She was strictly no-nonsense when she informed Gina that she was arranging to transport her to an all-girls boarding school. Her intentions were to enroll her there for the next three years.

The tidings stirred Gina and the expression that crossed her face conveyed confusion. She had been shuffled around so often, like an old shoe, it's no wonder she would feel as she did. Miss Jacobs sat hunched and almost flush against the steering wheel of her car as she drove. She never uttered a word and if ever she were to part with a smile, Gina feared her face would crack. Gina had noted, that whenever she irritated another driver, she would mumble, "Horse manure!" and wipe her hooked nose in defiance. It tickled Gina and she would grin.

They rode what seemed for hours and Gina was beginning to doze. "We're here," Miss Jacobs, startled her awake. "This boarding school is called Kremor. Can you remember that?"

"Yes, Miss Jacobs." Gina's eyes wandered curiously. She sighted many tan brick buildings, some with steeples; Dozens of tall, barren trees, that still wore snow, were situated all around the spacious grounds. It added distinction to the establishment; although the high, black iron gate and high fencing that hedged around the realty, hinted confinement; other than a boarding school.

Hurriedly, Miss Jacobs led her into the main building and into a spacious office that stenches of disinfectants. The office was cluttered with many high, dark green cabinets that were lined flush against the walls; numerous desks were lined in sequence in two separate rows. Above each desk, a light suspended from the ceiling that swayed eerily.

Gina set two, large paper bags, containing her belongings on the floor, then neared a divided railing. Catching her eye, was a short plump woman, wearing a long dark green dress; just looking at her deadpan face frightened the crap out of her. The sharp, rigor tone in the woman's voice when she addressed herself as Miss Adler; the administrator, surely stifled her.

"This is Gina Haskol the orphan we'd discussed. Miss Jacobs informed tactlessly and placed a folder At the top of the railing.

"Come here, Miss Prissy," Miss Adler called her and she warily shied over to her. Miss Adler leaned forward and Gina gawked inquisitively; at her twitching, gray bushy eyebrows and narrowed piercing black eyes. It gave Gina the jitters. Staring eye to eye, Miss Adler shook her stubby finger right under Gina's nose and said, "You'll behave in this school or we have ways to punish. Remember it good." She stood upright fussing at her dress.

Gina was speechless and her green eyes moistened. Gina turned to look behind and noticed that Miss Jacobs was gone. Suddenly, she sensed loneliness and felt lost in her new environment.

In dismay, Gina wandered over to a chair in the waiting area and wrestled her petite frame upon it. She sat with her hands folded in her lap and dangled her skinny legs waiting in silence. Many thoughts kept popping into Gina's head, but she hadn't concentrated on any particular one. Yet, she did wonder why Miss Adler had called her Miss Prissy. She didn't like the name and thought it was a dumb name.

Soon, a younger-looking woman with the hugest, bulging brown eyes that Gina had ever seen entered into the office. The woman was attired in a long, light and dark green dress.

"Miss Prissy," Miss Adler called gruffly.

"There goes that dumb name again," Gina whispered to herself hopping out of her chair.

"Miss Prissy, this is Miss Orr. She is one of the nursemaids who monitors the girls and she will take you to the dormitory and appoint your sleeping quarters." Miss Adler informed. Then both women mingled and gabbed about Gina being an orphan and troublesome. They labeled her surplus trash.

Perceiving the cruel rejection, Gina couldn't understand their unreasonable attitudes. She felt crushed hearing them belittle her to the lowest level.

C'mon, you! If you have anything with you, collect it and let's go." Miss Orr spoke annoyed.

Hastily, Gina picked up the two paper bags off the floor. She was having the hardest time holding them. They'd sag in the middle and she'd struggle to straighten them. Miss Orr looked on frowning displeasingly.

As they exited one of the buildings; the silence became distressing and to break the ice, Gina bravely sputtered, "Miss Orr, why is everybody so unfriendly?" She looked up at her, and Miss Orr scowled, dismissing her question, then began to walk a faster pace, and Gina skipped lively to keep up.

They entered an adjacent building and began to climb a steel staircase. It led them into a wide lengthy hallway composed of white and brown marble flooring with beige painted walls. Each step they took seemed to create thunderous echoes, deafening the ears. They walked midway when Miss Orr halted in front of doors that had sizable, rounded windows. She clumsily pushed in the swinging doors, allowing Gina to enter before her.

Gina couldn't believe she was seeing such a vast room, and when glancing around, she viewed a multitude of beds, dressers, nightstands, and lamps; Pale green drapes hung from the windows that were apart, allowing the daylight to peep through.

The girls were babbling and lingering about when Miss Orr checked their attention. She readily pointed at Gina and openly unloaded, "Girls! This is Gina and she's an orphan. She'll be here a long time. Dismissed!"

The girls sneered at Gina as if she were some kind of a freak. Without warning, they went haywire, berserk and began to ridicule her faded short dress, her shabby shoes, and her lengthy braids. It almost brought tears to her saddened eyes.

As she tailed Miss Orr to the far end corner of the dormitory, the heckling and why those girls hadn't been scolded, preyed on her mind; also Miss Orr's deceptive behavior which, she thought was needless.

"The bed, dresser, footlocker, and everything here is yours permanently." Miss Orr pointed out "You'll change your bed sheets every Friday! You'll make up your bed each morning before breakfast! And no pictures on the walls! Understood?" Gina nodded her head between the two paper bags and Miss Orr sped off.

With a sigh of relief, she placed the bags on the bed, beginning to unpack when promptly, a loud bell sounded, jarring her. Suddenly, the girls stampeded, like a herd of cattle, and retrieved seemingly, their uniformed winter jackets. They made a headlong rush for the swinging doors hollering, "It's chow time! It's chow time!"

Gina's eyes sidled, tiring, watching them all file out. She couldn't imagine what was happening, except that a fire drill might be in progress, remembering her first fire drill in first grade.

She wasn't hip to the girl's droll lingo, and curiously, she thought to lag behind them. Through the hallway, then down the stairway and out the building she ran, puffing. The cold air engulfed her, and she took a coughing spell that slowed her down. Luckily, she spotted the last two or three girls entering the third building. She ran to catch up, and finally indoors, she arrived at an oversized doorway that was already open. Catching her breath, she eyed the largeness of the room; it being equipped with scores of tables and chairs. She inhaled a delicious aroma of food and the thought dawned on her. "It's chow time! Yeah! That's what they meant," she muttered.

Alertly, she thought to stand in line, as the girls, when she felt her shoulder being yanked from behind. "Ouch!" she squealed and turned around to face her offender, but all she saw was bulging hips.

She tilted her head upwards, and saw what appeared to be a gigantic pudgy giant, with beady brown eyes and a flabby double chin that quivered like a roosters gill... and Gina froze.

"Hey, orphan! I'm Diane! I'm ten, like most of the dummies here. Some are younger, and I'm including the other two dormitories. As for me, I'm known as "IT" around here. Get it?" She pounced at her flabby boobs, braggingly. "So get your little butt out of here. Now! Me and my dummy pals were here first."

Diane pushed her out of line, and she obeyed too scared to refuse. She was befuddled, and after sizing up Diane, she didn't have to bother telling Gina she was "IT!" Gina was no dummy.....by no means.

When it came her turn to be served, a stocky woman with graying hair tied in a bun spoke from behind the counter. "I'm Fanny, chief cook and bottle washer," her brown eyes scanned Gina. "So you're the orphan kid them gals were yakking about! I sure can tell you," she sighed. "Them gals don't like you! You're an orphan--an outsider. Them gals say, you look like you just got off the banana boat. You just don't fit in with the ritzy!" exploded into a hearty laughter and Gina pondered at her confused. "I'll say it again, kid! They don't like you, so look out! The sparks will fly!" she flipped a glob or watery spinach atop of her mashed potatoes, then shooed her off to hunt a table to sit at.

Each time Gina tried to settle at a table, the girls acted like they were the "Cat's Meow" and would jointly spout, "No orphans allowed! This seat is taken! Scram kid!"

Skedaddle she did; gloomily silent and disturbed. She hadn't expected the cold-shoulder treatment. She'd always been a compatible child and these unforeseen dilemma's that keep popping up, had got her bugged.

She spotted Miss Orr monitoring, and confronted her, relating the objections.

"The girls; more-or-less do as they please." Miss Orr said. "You orphans! Always complaining and looking for attention." She took off and Gina scurried behind her thinking wildly, why had Miss Orr said what she did, knowing full well, it wasn't true. Gina was only looking for companionship. "I'll assign you this unoccupied table permanently."

"All the time? Can anyone sit with me when I make friends?"

"No! You'll sit alone and keep out of trouble. The girls behind you will befriend you." She looked to them with a cynical look in those beaming eyes or hers, simpering slyly.

Gina took note that her neighbors were Diane and some or her dummy friends. They were all decked out in their hoity-toity clothes and smirking snobbishly at her. She wisely chose to sit furthest away, near the side aisle, adjacent to a closed door.

She cringed, her dainty face sick-like, staring at her food that looked like mush, when Fanny's upsetting words returned to haunt her. The proud feeling she experienced seemed to have faded away and fear set in its place. Her thoughts racked with uncertainties, and why being an orphan has caused so much discord.

"Hey, orphan," a voice growled, hindering her thoughts. She glanced around and saw Diane bad slid her chair, close enough to hers, and snatched her chocolate milk.

"That's mine," Gina reached for the glass container.

"Heck if it is... orphan!" Diane shoved her arm aside, then began gulping and dribbling down her blubbering chin; and Gina thought her a slobbering hog.

When lunchtime was over, the girls recessed outdoors to the playground. Denoting the jackets, Gina was gratified that she hadn't removed hers.

The girls were hellish as all get out. They would not let Gina partake in any games or permit her to sway on a swing. They treated her as if she had contracted the plague. She was a greenhorn. She was vulnerable and an orphan and those snooty tykes let her know it.

She felt renounced. She wanted to play too!

She sat herself on the cold ground in front of a little shed, shivering in her shrunken jacket. She spied a little girl playing alone, in a sandbox and she thought to make a friend. She rose from her sitting position, nearing the little girl. "Can I play with you?" The little girl looked up at Gina with her bright blue eyes, seemingly ready to speak when Diane and several older girls dashed over to them.

Because Diane threw her weight around, and what she said goes, she had threatened all the girls to stay away from the orphan, or else! She showed her fist.

Gina went her separate way, and the entire afternoon played alone, in another sandbox. She sulked about why everybody was so mean to her; and why being an orphan has caused everybody to dislike her. She wished Diane would stop calling her orphan. Her mind was messing up and she couldn't understand anything. She was becoming uncomfortably cold as the sun began to fade beneath the clouds. She wanted to burrow herself under the sand, when a loud bell sounded, as earlier.

The girls flew off like a swarm of bees and Gina shadowed them, welcoming the indoors. It was suppertime, and she was itching for a hot, hearty meal.

Devious Diane had other thoughts, when she chose to pull a dangerous prank by pulling Gina's chair out from under her and she fell to the floor. As if that wasn't enough, she purposely dropped the chair atop of her, and it came crashing noisily to the floor. She lay hurting and crying.

Miss Orr, was "Johnny on the spot" pulling her out from under the table. She glared down at her with those jutting eyeballs of hers and began dispraising her. She accused her of being a menace and creating a ruckus. Slow in picking herself up, Gina refuted the accusation, and was swatted across the face for rebutting. She was sent off without any supper to prepare for bed. She fled crying, and deafening her ears was the girl's foolish laughter.

Gina's mind weighed heavy in thought as she hustled about finishing the unpacking she'd left undone. She was angry and hurt. There was no one to talk with. She was lonely and gripped with mixed emotions. She wondered why Miss Orr had stuck her in this loony bin they call a boarding school. She came across her tattered nightgown and put it on. For all she cared, she'd go to bed in her undies.

She settled on the floor near the heated radiator, which occasionally clunked crazily. She was coloring and enjoying the serenity of the moment.

Shortly, the girls shuffled into the dormitory, wild as lunatics. Diane wasted no time noticing Gina's tattered nightgown, insulting her. Suddenly, she began to bounce crazily waving her arms shuttle wise. The floor began to tremble and Gina thought for sure it would cave in. Diane started yelling and whistling, quieting the girls then said, "Let's nickname the orphan, Little Orphan Annie, just like the comics in the newspaper. What do you think dummies?"

"Yeah! Zowie! Hot dog!" the dummies harmonized in their crazy lingo.

"Okay, I'll be right back." She marched all of her blubber over to the lone washstand. She filled a glass with water, then stomped herself back over to Gina. Uncaringly, she poured the water atop of Gina's head. "It's a rebirth in your honor, Little Orphan Annie." She cooed.

Soaked, Gina backed away screaming. "Why are you doing this? Why do you keep picking on me and hurting me? I didn't do anything to you!"

"Cause, I found you make a terrific patsy for my bored moments, and it ain't ending here!" she cocked her head impishly and stuck her tongue out. "You're an orphan! You clash with us girls. We got the bucks--the moolah--the money, and you ain't got a pot to pee in. We don't like outsiders." She fixed her hands upon those bulky hips of hers and awkwardly about faced, then stuck her rump plum in Gina's face. Gina sat wide-eyed and motionless and swore she was seeing the tail-end of an elephant.

She used the edge of the bedspread to wipe the wetness from her person, then put away her coloring book and crayons. She felt chilled, and climbed into bed, covering herself entirely. She was wrought with doubts. The phrase, "The sparks will fly," stuck in her mind. She wondered fearfully what prevailed. She fell asleep to the sound of the girl's gibberish voices gabbing foolhardily.

CHAPTER TWO

Gina had to learn and fend on her own. The sound of a bell means "hop to it." There is no dilly--dallystuff for her or she is punished.

Miss Adler and Miss Orr have remained evasive. Worse, yet, they wear a cord tied around their waists from which hangs a handy ruler. They use it to lash Gina unnecessarily.

Gina couldn't understand why she hasn't been assigned to regular classes as the other girls. She had questioned Miss Adler about it, and she jumped down her throat, telling her not to concern herself.

She spends each day in the library alone, reading, coloring, but mostly thinking. Many times, she has fallen asleep at the library table from sheer boredom. It is the sharp sting from a ruler slapping against her flesh that awakens her. She'd tried to explain, time after time, that she's lonely and didn't know she'd fallen asleep. She wants to be in class and learn. Then for disputing, she is lashed.

She has been unable to reckon why the girls never call one another by their first names. It seems, they all prefer to call each other dummy, moron, or by some other slang term. It has baffled her as to how each girl knows who is calling whom. She has been unable to attach a name to any girl except Diane. The faculty of the establishment address the girls endearingly, and Gina ... they treat her like the trash and the outsider everybody claims her to be.

She wishes that weekends never existed when all the girl's parents visit them, filling her thoughts with wishful thinking. Consistently, she'll sneak up a side aisle of the spacious auditorium. Unnoticed, she'll hide behind one of the maroon velvet drapes which hang from the high windows and inconspicuously, peek around the drape. Enviously, she'll watch the girls happily open the gifts that their parents had brought for them. When she heard some of the girls throw verbal fits because they were displeased with their presents, she would anger. She couldn't imagine anyone being ungrateful.

When she'd absorbed all she could stand, she'd shy away into the vestibule of the auditorium then walk over to the candy concession stand. She'd drool at the sight of the girls biting into a candy bar, and spitefully, they would flaunt it in her face, tantalizingly, Feeling dejected, she'd disappear and wander to the dormitory, crying her heart out.

From the first day Gina had arrived on the scene in this loco school, that numb-head Diane, and some of her dummy pals had taunted her every chance they got. In a few short months, they had about driven her nutty.

Diane must have laid awake nights straining that so-called brain of hers, plotting something crazy; even if it was only to drop a glass on the floor, breaking it. She'd work up a sweat tracking down Miss Orr, then tell her some cock-and-bull story that Gina was the culprit. Poor Gina... She was helpless and wound up getting whipped then having to clean up the mess.

Diane had to be "Bats in her belfry" the day she had sneaked dead cockroaches in between the sheets of Gina's bed. Those dummies split their seams laughing as Gina went ape and pooped her pants.

According to the calendar on the library wall, it was April Fools' Day and Gina's eighth birthday; it had been circled in red. Classes had been dismissed for the day and Gina headed for the dormitory. Inside the dormitory, the chatter was moderate. The girls seemed to have their eyes fixed on Gina as she walked over to her area and found her bed gone...

Her eyes just about popped out of her head. She was flustered and thought she'd gone coo-coo. Excitedly, she questioned the girls and they played "smart aleck" until Diane opened her yap. "PoorLittle Orphan Annie! Her bed's gone! Now ain't that a shame" She tut-tutted. "Hey, dummies! Which one of you thieves swiped the bed?"

"I did," a girl chuckled.

"No, you didn't! I did!" another girl claimed.

Miss Orr had entered the dormitory, making her usual four o'clock round. In a flash, fat Diane galloped over to her yelling, "Miss Orr! Miss Orr! That orphan kid pushed her bed all the way over to the other end of the room!" she fibbed. "She said she wanted a change. I told her to leave the bed where it was, but she wouldn't listen."

"That's not true!" Gina cried as Miss Orr treaded over to her. "I didn't," Miss Orr warded her off with a walloping slap in the face.

"That was for retorting! Now get your fanny over to that bed and start pushing." She lashed at Gina's legs as she ran crying.

She braced herself against the dark brass railing of the bed. She shoved and strained; huffing and puffing. She was such a little tot; even the huge pots in the kitchen seemed bigger than she; and now this. The bed sat on white porcelain rollers. As she pushed, it squealed and swiveled. When she tugged, it screeched and swirled. The bed seemed to have a mind of its own as it repeated its course to its respective abode. The dummies had a wing-ding time of it all. They sounded like a bunch of "screaming meemies" and hopped like Jack Rabbits. It sickened Gina and she wanted to shout for all to "shut up!"

She was bushed, and sat herself on the edge of the bed, when Miss Orr thought to inspect it. "And since when do you make up a bed with the sheet over the spread?" she struck Gina repeatedly and blood seeped through her skin. "How dare you defy rules! Get this bed made up properly."

Gina wiped the blood off with the skirt or her dress and obediently obeyed. She ached all over. Poor kid... She didn't know it she was coming or going. Her tears drained as she lay on her bed, sullenly nursing her wounds.

"Hot-diggerty-damn! Happy April Fools' Day, Little Orphan Annie." Diane shot off her mouth.

"Hey, dummies, we had that timed perfect, didn't we?"

"Yeah! Sure did! It was a blast!" the dummies singed out.

"Hey, Diane!" a dummy kid called. "You sure can fast talk and twist things around. Miss Orr believes anything you tell her.

"Yeah! And that's the way I like it!"

The supper bell sounded and those dummies scattered like monkeys, out the swinging door. Gina had had it and remained in bed. She was in a festering mood; something that she'd never had to brave with until she'd come to this crazy school. She got to thinking ill-naturedly about Diane weighing a ton, and how she had to turn sideways to squeeze through a doorway. It's lucky there are swinging doors, she thought. She ought to brush those crooked teeth of hers too! Her breath stinks so bad it's a wonder those dummy pals of hers don't think she pooped her pants and was wearing them on the wrong end. She's so dirty looking and looks like a big rhino. She wished that all the girls would choke on their food.

From a happy-go-lucky child, Gina had turned hateful and despised everyone. She'd never known herself to mock or hurt anyone. Those girls were slowly destroying her. The frustrations she bore weigh heavy and there was no one to talk to, but the four walls.

Easter morning, the bells tolled melodiously from the steeple. Gina peered out the window, admiring nature's beauty and thinking it was just another day for her. She held a deep-seeded resentment as she watched the girls "Putting on the Ritz" parading around the dormitory. They were swanked up in their new fancy and frilly outfits, and she was dressed like a rag picker. While the girls waited for their parents to arrive and escort them to some lavish restaurant, they gabbed about who was going to get the biggest Easter basket or chocolate rabbit.

"Hey, Little Orphan Annie! Where are you going today looking like a hobo?" Diane taunted. "And who's going to bring you a chocolate rabbit?"

"Hah! She'll probably wind up with the rabbits' turds!" a girl chided then they all left howling.

The days were zooming by, and on the agenda, was a musical festival. It was scheduled for the end of the first half of the school semester, and Gina being the outcast (although, she was permitted to attend the girls evening rehearsal.) It wasn't through the goodness of their hearts however... it was just another means of torment.

Every evening, she would sit in the rear of the auditorium, darkened, but with spotlights illuminating the stage. She watched several of the girls enact a scene from the book <u>LITTLE WOMEN</u>.

They were forever bungling their lines and clowning around. They would giggle and act like jerks; kind of swatting playfully at one another. Diane held role of "Jo" who in the book is supposedly an ardent bookworm and Gina couldn't imagine Diane a bookworm.

One girl played a classical melody on the piano and another, sang the song "When Irish Eyes Are Smiling." She warbled so high pitched and off key it bent Gina's ears.

The acts were numerous and the more Gina attended evening rehearsal, the more she yearned to take part; it being a great satisfaction to the girls. Rather than contend with her desires, she'd choose to go to bed.

During the span of time that evening rehearsal had been taking place the girls had also been engrossed in their studies for the scheduled end-term examinations. Breakfast, lunch and supper, they had their snoots crammed in the pages of their texts and for Gina it was a welcome blessing. It favored a slight reprieve from harassment for her.

The evening for the presentation of the musical festival was on the roll. From backstage, Gina watched the girls nervously dress in the costumes, befitting their renditions. They were jumpy and running around, like chickens with their heads cut off.

"Loan me a comb, moron!"

"I want it next, goon!"

"Hey, goofy! Come hook this fool dress up for me!" Diane barked. "This darn hoop! It keeps swinging and bumping every which way."

"Pucker up your lips, dummies! I'm ready to smear the lipstick on your yaps." A girl hollered.

Gina listened alertly, as the girls were paging one another by slang names when, out of the blue, the notion hit her. She was finally able to reckon how those girls knew who was calling whom; accounting that each girl had a slang name of their very own, but whenever a group of girls were addressed, then the term dummy was used. At least, Gina thought, she wasn't altogether loco.

The girls screeching voices pierced in Gina's ears, that she could hardly think straight, when she decided to take off for the auditorium. She was feeling depressed, and crossly thought about the girls, thinking they looked like beauty queens, she'd seen in magazines; But they looked more like silly elves. She thought about fat Diane in that wide hooped, long skirt looking like a bloated cow, and her thinking she looks like a dainty prima donna.

When Gina arrived in the auditorium, the families and friends of the girls were seating themselves. Her eyes goggled in awe, noticing the women all spruced up in their flashy finery of silks, satins and taffeta. They wore gaudy hats that were trimmed with colorful feathers, ribbons, and veils. Their gems knocked the eyeballs out of her, as they glistened and sparkled like the rainbow. They were the elite and wallowed in wealth. The "mullah" as Diane had put it.

The lights dimmed and colorful spotlights flashed on, circling the entire front of the stage. As Gina viewed those whippersnappers, at their best, it was difficult for her to believe that they were the same nasty brats she saw every day.

When the performance had come to its finale, the ovation was overwhelming. From backstage, the girls appeared. They ran and skipped about, seeking out their families and friends. Tender hugs and kisses described a job well done. Gina saddened, sighting all the affection being doled. She also craved for a kind word and a warm embrace, but there was no fooling herself. There was no one to love her.

A banquet was being held in the cafeteria for all to feast. The guests stood in a line along three long tables covered with bright yellow tablecloths. On top of the tables, there were platters that had been set with an assortment of meats, various salads, baked goodies and beverages. At times, Fanny popped out of the kitchen with a fresh batch of food, and Gina's taste buds watered while her eyes were getting bigger than her stomach.

After everyone had served themselves, Gina thought to indulge, picking up a platter. Unexpectedly, Miss Orr approached her, snatching her plate. "What do you think you're doing? This food is not meant for you! You didn't participate in the festival. Therefore, you're not entitled! Get yourself up to the dormitory immediately."

Tearfully, she obeyed but was unable to understand Miss Orr's objection. How much food could she have eaten, she thought? She couldn't help that the girls wouldn't let her in the show. As she stepped outdoors, the warm night air seemed to sooth her frustration. She wished she could stay outdoors and rest on the soft grass all night. She gazed at a silvery moon and millions of shiny, twinkling stars, thinking how pretty they were and wished hard upon one.

Within the dormitory, one amber light bulb, which set above the swinging doors, was lit. The room was dark and eerie. Gina began imagining seeing ugly faces appearing out of nowhere, frightening her. Quickly, she fled over to her nightstand, turning on the lamp light and felt safer.

She prepared for bed, when her thoughts drifted to Miss Orr's unjust behavior.   She could have permitted Gina to eat. There was plenty of food. She was so hungry, but even so, she wouldn't have eaten much. Why is she so mean to Gina and always so" lovey-dovey" with the girls?   Oh, how she wished she were elsewhere. Someplace where someone would love her, she told herself, saddened.

Later, the ceiling lights were flicked on and the girls noisily barged into the dormitory. Those who were venturing home for the summer vacation hooted and hollered the loudest when retrieving their luggage and what a hullaballoo that was. They screamed and shouted like maniacs. They bobbed and weaved crazily amongst themselves as each girl tried to bid a last ado to a dummy friend.

CHAPTER THREE

Before breakfast, Gina counted within (her dormitory), eighteen girls, out of thirty, who had remained behind. Diane was one of them and that was disastrous for Gina. With Diane around, she'd never make any friends and often wondered, if there were any girls in the (three dormitories) who would befriend her if not for Diane's constant threats.

Diane was glum and "dead as a dodo" without her favorite dummy pals. Not a single day could pass without her drumming up, in that fool head of hers, something foul, in conflict with Gina.

Gina always played alone, in a sandbox and Diane had her pinpointed. Whenever a brainstorm hit her, she'd make a beeline for Gina pestering the hell out of her. She'd whack and cuss at her. She'd forever get her dander up, for no reason, and spit at her from in between the spacing of her yellowed front teeth, then tug and knot her long braids.

A whim struck her, this one day, when she'd sneaked up behind Gina and planted the skeleton of a dead snake on her shoulder. Gina took one look and went batty, trying to shake the dang thing off.

The nursemaids, when on duty, monitoring, could care less what happens to her. It seems they see no evil, hear no evil, and speak no evil, and in their eyes, Diane could do no wrong. Just like the day when she stood in front of Gina, in a shifty manner. She was holding a bottle filled with some kind of a brownish color, soda mixture. She kept shaking the stuff and it sizzled, bubbled and foamed. The bottle had an odd looking cap which she'd kept a tight hold when suddenly, like a champion soda-jerker, she sprayed Gina royally. Exasperated, Gina high-tailed after her, but stopped in her tracks realizing the senselessness of it all. Retracing her steps, she sat down to dry in the sun. Two hours later, her clothing and braids were stiff as boards.

Gina was mentally fatigued. She'd even wondered if hiding up a tree would be safe with Diane around. She was up a blind alley and nowhere to go, but fat Diane knew; especially when she had blended a mixture of dirt and water to a thick texture, in a large bucket. She and some dummy friends, had crept up behind Gina and toppled the stuff all over her. She was a goopy sight. Those girls had done her in then scooted off laughing the heck out of themselves.

A nursemaid, standing near-by, witnessed the incident and hadn't troubled herself to say boo. She caught Miss Orr's attention and she hurriedly rushed over and began lashing at her for making such an awful mess or herself. She cried bitterly, but there wasn't any getting around to the truth with Miss Orr. Her punishment was dry in the hot sun and she wound up stiff as starch.

Diane was a "sicko" along with all the other girls who had joined in her crusade, intimidating. Gina hated Diane. She wanted to claw at her and grind her to a pulp, but frightened of her monstrous size, could only wish her bad things.

On a certain, hot, sunny day, Gina had been playing alone, in the sandbox, when the elastic band of her panties had torn apart. She tried to knot both ends, but the elastic shredded. "I know! I'll go to the office and get a pin." She muttered.

"Hey, dummies! Look over here!" she heard a voice shrill. "Little Orphan Annie dropped her drawers to take a pee and her butt is hanging out."

Gina irked watching the girls come charging over as if they were in a running marathon, out-racing the other. They cackled at her nudity when someone from behind booted her in the rear and she went sailing to the other end of the sandbox, landing embarrassingly. Crying in shame, she struggled picking herself and her panties up simultaneously, then waddled away listening to those dummies resonant laughter fade in the distance.

Miss Adler was exiting her office when Gina anxiously approached her. "My rubber broke on my panties. May I please have a pin to fix them?" Gina asked.

A whopping smack across Gina's face rocked her. "That was for forgetting who I am." Miss Adler spoke arrogantly. "I am Miss

Adler. So that you will not forget it in the future, you will hold your panties up yourself for the remainder of the day. Now go! Leave my presence!"

Dumbfounded, she sped crying, not knowing which way to turn, and feeling like the little black sheep that lost its way. She wouldn't return to the playground; only to be teased, she thought and chose to be alone.

Holding her panties, she walked along the pavements surrounding the many buildings when she came across a dead-end. She spotted an old, dilapidated, abandoned house and elected to sit on its front porch steps. She viewed acres of open fields and lavished the tranquility it beheld.

Thenceforth, the remainder or the summer, that old house became her refuge and sphere of activity. On stormy days, it was back into the library, wishing the rain would go away.

The last day of summer vacation had rolled around. The girls and, particularly Diane, were restless and fired-up awaiting nightfall, when the vacationers would be returning. When they did, all hell broke loose. Gina was in dire need of earplugs. When they finally simmered down, Diane monopolized their attention and began, batting the breeze, about all the spiteful jokes she had pulled on Gina.

Gina wondered if Diane would ever come up for air, and wished she could muzzle that prune looking, fat motor mouth of hers.

At breakfast, Diane kept hopping out of her chair, like a yo-yo, hounding and socking at Gina. She was beginning to feel like a punching bag. When Diane tired, she jabbed Gina's arm with a fork and then, swiped her milk along with a buttered roll. Gina held a stiff upper lip, churning within. She could guess that Diane was showing off to remind her dummy friends that she was still "IT."

The second half of the semester was on the move and once again, the library had become Gina's sanctuary. Miss Adler and Miss Orr take turns playing their never-ending game, policing her. She survives the same "hum-drum" routine daily. She is not permitted outdoors when classes are in session she feels confined and deprived. She yearns to sway on a swing, but knows the chance will never come. She has become stagnant and is losing a grip on herself. Loneliness is driving her crazy and her mind, at times, ready to snap.

Her thoughts are usually preoccupied with the outdoors. She's constantly gazing out a window discontentedly, watching, Mother Nature let the soft green grass wilt and blanket it with snow.

Diane and her dummy friends dominate the evenings and continue to conjure their evil conspiracies, getting their kicks at Gina's expense.

Thanksgiving Day had crept up and the aroma of turkey surely filled Gina's nostrils as she entered the cafeteria. She was remembering all the Thanksgivings she'd spent in different foster homes, and how that day had been celebrated with a huge turkey and all the trimmings. Fanny had dished her out a plate of food that looked like slop for the hogs and it broke Gina's spirit.

She was feeling melancholy, and as she walked the center aisle, a girl had intentionally stuck out her foot in Gina's path. Suddenly, in one fell swoop, her lengthy braids flew, sticking straight up, then tray and all she went sprawling to the floor. Stunned, she laid on her stomach, looking about, and heard all those idiot girls laughing up a storm. She tried to pick herself up, but kept slipping and sliding and wound up against the leg of a table, landing on her rear.

She caught a glimpse of Miss Orr eyeballing her and, she stiffened. She was petrified. "You clumsy, ornery, child! Is there anything you do correctly?" Miss Orr screeched.

She was agitated and after Gina's hide. Carefully, she tip-toed through the slop when suddenly, all Gina saw was the color green soaring by. Miss Orr had taken a spill, flopping awkwardly on her back side. It was chaos! Her chubby race turned white as a sheet and the girls broke into fits of hysterical laughter, shedding tears.

Even Gina laughed eyeing Miss Orr sitting stupefied and motionless. Her bold eyes seemed rolling in her head and her two front teeth hung lazed. She wasn't amused by no means and began shouting at Gina, ordering her to the kitchen to clean off then return to clean the mess. Miss Orr was a mess herself and she angered at Gina more so.

Gina utilized the table aiding herself to her feet and as she streaked by Miss Orr, the girls began acting real "dippy," ranting at her offensive appearance.

Fanny had the look of an embittered hag as she filled up an enormous slop sink with soapy water, and roughly leaned Gina over it. The sink was so high that she stood on her tippy-toes. As Fanny kept pushing her further to meet the water, Gina felt herself folding in half. She began to cough and gasp for air. Fanny pulled out a large sponge from out or the water and plopped it atop of Gina's head. Fanny bellowed like a cow as Gina felt the sudsy water seep into her ears, run down her face and into her eyes. In a flash, she backed away from the sink hobbling crazily and screaming, "Fanny! My eyes! They burn bad! It's the soap! 'Why did you do that?"

"Okay, kid! You can stop play acting!" Fanny jerked Gina's head back dabbing the wetness from all over. "Serves you right, kid! You're the cause for Miss Orr's fall! So, it's one way to teach you not to go around spilling trays. I slaved over a hot stove all morning. It's bad enough you spill and break everything else around here."

The sting had slackened and although not fully recovered from her setback, Fanny sent her off to the cafeteria which had been vacated. She fetched the cleaning implements and while in the process of mopping, a surge of resentment hovered her mind. It seemed she had asked herself a million times. Why does she get blamed for everything and get beat? Why won't anyone listen to her? Why does she have to be an orphan? Why was she put in this horrible place? But there were no answers and never would be.

End-term examinations were uppermost in the girl's minds and also the upcoming Christmas holiday. In the evenings, the girls studied diligently and limited Diane having her usual field days tormenting Gina. This was a pleasing respite for her. Occasionally, a girl would pipe up with an off-beat joke or a zany riddle. At times, they would jibber-jabber about the gifts they wanted for Christmas and then, it was back to the text books.

Snowflakes and freezing temperatures were at its peak and the Christmas holiday had descended. Colorfully illuminated Christmas trees set in all areas of the establishment. Pine wreaths hung from the doors and windows, creating a cheerful atmosphere.

A vast display that was situated in a corner of the vestibule of the auditorium was most impressionable to Gina. She had overheard some of the girls refer to it as the "nativity scene.

The display featured a huge rounded cave like shelter. Within the cave set a lifelike baby wrapped in a white blanket, lying in a straw bed. Two lifelike cows lay on either side of the straw bed. A misty cloud of vapor was sporadically ejected from the cow's mouth, which depicted warmth from their breath for the baby. There were lifelike statues of a man and woman beside the cows, kneeling. Above the entrance of the shelter was suspended a burning lantern, accenting the scene.

Gina was unfamiliar with the story or background of the nativity scene, except that she had overheard that a notable infant was born on Christmas Eve and its birth was celebrated throughout the world each year.

There is magic in the thought of Christmas, but for Gina it only held emptiness and heartache. Somberly, she watched the girls hustling and bustling about in the auditorium, engrossing themselves in one another's gifts and munching on goodies. She felt so alone--so abandoned, and all she yearned for was a taste of a candy cane or a little cookie.

Scheduled, was a two week Christmas holiday recess. The girls who had remained in school, which included Diane, occupied their time in the newly erected gymnasium. Gina had occupied her time in the library.

Gossip had it that Diane was on an exercise kick. She was planning to lose weight, was the word. It hadn't proved anything to Gina whenever she'd swipe her food. She was all hogwash.

The dismal days lagged on. Gina would wish it were springtime, remembering the old house, fields and meadows, and the peace of mind it held for her.

On one of those dismal days, she thought to pry and had entered the gymnasium. She sat alone on a long bench situated on the sidelines.   She'd loved to have challenged the activities when, her eyes wandered to the ropes hanging from the ceiling to a huge mat below. She spied Diane, some of her pals and several other hulky girls, gyrating about. They were panting and shaking like jelly. Diane caught a glimpse of her and scowled, looking like a hideous witch, then charged over to her like an enraged bull.

"Who the hell do you think you're looking at? I saw you grinning at me!" Diane snorted. "I ought to use you for a punching bag just for looking! I don't like being stared at!"

"I wasn't staring at you! I was looking at everybody." Gina retorted.

"Ah, don't hand me that bologna!" she let loose with a fierce punch to Gina's chest, causing her to topple backwards on to the floor. "That ought to teach you not to stare at me! You creep!"

Gina's chest felt numb and brooding, she ran to the library telling herself she shouldn't have been so nosey. Oh, how she despised that Diane. She wished she could run away! Far away!

Came the New Year and preparation for the second semester was in order. "Oh, to think!" Diane hollered loudly awakening everyone. "Another two years in this dump!" She yawned offensively noisy.

"Well, Diane!" a girl spoke sleepily. "You'll still have Little Orphan Annie to amuse you."

"Yeah! I guess I will!" She spoke in a boorish manner.

Heeding Diane's words, Gina swallowed hard, dreading having to remain in this God forsaken place. Her tears and bruises remind her of the hate she holds for everyone. She is extremely lonely, cries often and resents being an orphan. She survives on gallant courage and in her reveries she pines for the mommy and daddy (whom she has never known).

CHAPTER FOUR

The latest gossip circling around the breakfast tables was the arrival at several nursemaids and a teacher. Finished with the little breakfast which Diane had so generously left Gina, she trotted on her usual route to the library.

"Miss Prissy," she heard Miss Adler call from behind and shuddered as she pivoted around, hastily scrambling over to her. "In the morning after breakfast you will be tutored by Miss Alexis in the spare room of the library." Gina caught her breath and supposed that Miss Alexis would be like everybody else; Mean and nasty!

In the library, she recovered her favorite book, "<u>GRIMM'S FAIRYTALES</u>." She loved the fantasy world she read about. It placed her in a beautiful dreamland, and she could escape from the cruelty around her.

During supper, aside from a few smut and vulgar remarks, and Diane swiping Gina's tapioca pudding, it went rather smoothly for a change, she thought. However, when clearing her tray suddenly, she felt crawling fingers reaching under her dress and her undies being pulled down to her feet. Startled, she looked behind and scanned lots of blubber sneaking off. "You fatso-head, Diane! Why did you do that?"

"Cause your ass!" Diane paused. "It looks better than your pickle-puss face. If your dresses get any shorter, nobody will have to pull your panties down. The show would be on you."

It was the first time Diane had ever made any sense. Gina faced the reality, humiliated, but the truth hadn't campaigned. Any love between them.

Activity in the dormitory was temperate until Diane hooted an earsplitting, hog-calling roar, that shook the place, then she yelled, "Hey, dummies! Got a wild idea!" she kneeled on her bed, nearly falling through. The girls hadn't paid much mind, when she yelled again, "Hey, Joyce, Janet, Tina. Come overhere! All you dummies."

The suckling's wiggling to the hog, Gina thought nastily. She was fluked hearing Diane call her dummy pals by their real names. They had crowded together, and she couldn't pin a name on anyone. Diane began whispering and waving her arms to beat the band.

Gina couldn't hear what they were saying, except for lots of giggling. Her senses told her that Diane was up to her wily tricks.

Soon, they scattered and began squealing, like they had dreadful bellyaches. They jumped and jogged maniacally, and nearing Gina's bed, altogether they chanted. "You ain't got no mommy! You ain't got no daddy! You're Little Orphan Annie and belong in some cranny!" Louder and louder they repeated rhythmically.

Gina stared at them half out of her wits. There was no place to run. "Leave me alone! You're all so mean! Go away! I hate you!" she cried and buried her face into her pillow.

Unexpectedly, everything deadened and the room fell eerily silent. Curiously, Gina lifted her head and strained to focus her blurry, tear-filled eyes. She saw standing in the doorway, showing anger upon her face a striking, tall fearless looking woman. She was attired in a long, dark green dress with a white trimmed collar.

The girls stood agape and wide-mouthed, frozen solid, as the woman heatedly denounced them up one side and down the other.

She was fiery, insisting on learning whom the girls were harassing; informing them that she'd heard them clear down the other end of the hallway.

Gina's little heart thumped wildly at the sound of her authoritative voice; although, the thought of those devils being scolded was phenomenal.

"Well! I am waiting for a response!" she gritted her teeth.

That demon Diane stepped forward, cramping her style, along with another girl who called herself Joyce. Her olive black eyes glared frigidly at the woman, and nervously, she kept tugging at her cauliflower ears. She glanced at Diane, and together they pointed at Gina. It amazed Gina that Diane would dare own up to anything and supposed it was her way to get rid of the woman. The woman appeared satisfied then introduced herself as Miss Alexis, a tutor, then shooed them off to their text books, "As it should be!" She stressed and they scampered in silence with their tails between their legs.

In the quietness of it all, it dawned on Gina that Miss Alexis, who had appeared out of nowhere, was to be her tutor. She didn't know what to think. She was scared. After all...she'd frightened her so. Her little heart was still palpitating faster than ever. But mysteriously, a strange feeling swept through her as Miss Alexis neared her. She couldn't understand what was happening to her. Miss Alexis no longer wore that mean, embittered expression on her face. She was wearing the face of an angel. Gina felt bewitched and supposed she was dreaming. Seemingly, a magnetism of sorts attracted her to Miss Alexis's sensitive blue eyes and warm, sweet smile. Oddly, she felt safe. Miss Alexis sat on the edge of the bed and voiced, "Are you Gina?" Her voice was mellow.

Gina hesitated momentarily. She was surprised to hear her real name (she had almost forgotten).

"Yes! How did you know my name? How did you know I was Gina?"

"Miss Adler. She described you as the littlest young lass here and, looking about me, I find that true. I'm Miss Alexis and I'm going to be your tutor."

Gina was confused. She was trying to get her head on straight convincing herself that anyone would be kind to her in this place. She depicted Miss Alexis as a fairy godmother who pops in and disappears just as quick.

Miss Alexis studied Gina intently, then said, "My, but you certainly look undernourished. You're nothing but skin and bones."

"That's because Diane, (one of the girls), swipes my food all the time." Gina blurted and passively babbled about some of the horrible goings-on. "Even on my birthday, It's April Fools' Day, they played a nasty joke and I got beat." Gina began to sob and Miss Alexis could only appear mortified.

Miss Alexis held Gina warmly in her arms, comforting and Gina felt she was in heaven. When her crying jag simmered, Miss Alexis versed to Gina that she couldn't be entirely in judgment of anyone not as yet anyway. However, she counseled Gina to be very strong; ignore the girls heckling and don't let them destroy her; hope for a better day and forgive your enemies. "Now my dear, get some sleep. See you in the morning." She darted off.

Gina felt aglow. Her cheeks felt flush thinking how gentle Miss Alexis had been. She wondered if she was only a dream or was she for real? Or was she just a figment of her imagination?

This exceptional morning was different from any other morning Gina had awakened to. She had to see Miss Alexis, and if she was really, real! Excited, she hurriedly tended her chores, evaded Diane's chronic hassling, and passing up breakfast, sped for the library. She slipped into the spare room and a blackboard resting on an easel caught her fancy, then she elected to sit nearest the desk and a long counter with cabinets below.

She sat fidgeting, impatiently, thinking! Thinking! Thinking! She heard the clacking of footsteps and she tensed. Miss Alexis had finally arrived and Gina was on "cloud nine" to see her wearing the same warm, sweet smile and hearing her mellow voice that she felt a burst for joy. Miss Alexis was for real, alive and beautiful!

Miss Alexis was quick to notice Gina's short dress. "I do believe you are in grave need of clothing, dear." She remarked. "Pity how things are shunned!"

They proceeded with the morning session and Miss Alexis took patience when instructing Gina her daily lessons. Gina was determined to learn. She favored spelling and definitions of words and Miss Alexis prepared special assignments in that category, to help her advance.

During lunch break, Gina felt nature call, entering the lavatory. Diane, her dummy pals, and other girls were sounding obnoxiously rowdy. They were holding rolls of toilet paper in their hands. Tiny wadded balls clung on the walls, on themselves, and everywhere. Gina summed up the situation and wasn't bound to stick around in the line of fire.

"How's Miss Alexis?" Joyce cooed.

Gina drowned her words; occupying one of the partitioned bathrooms when the girls began buzzing like bees, then began splashing water at one another.

Out of the blue, Diane shrieked, "Whoop-de-do! I gotta' take a crap! Wait up! Don't do anything!" the partition door slammed shut and, just as quick, she laid this terrific fart, that rattled everyone; and Gina thought for sure it would blow her right off the bowl; along with the atrocious stink that nearly keeled her over. Golly-gee… that was a stinkeroo… it was rotten, Gina thought grinning.

Diane had exited her latrine and when Gina was preparing to exit hers, she saw beneath the partition feet closing in on her and suddenly, felt something wet showering on the top of her head, alarming her. She felt her head feeling soggy wet globs of toilet paper.

"This batch is from all of us for Miss Alexis!" the dummies hollered and another barrage of the soggy stuff rained all over her.

"You dumb baboons!" Gina shouted, provoked, as they noisily raced out the door. "They can't even let me alone when I'm tinkling! Now, I'm all wet and cold!" she mumbled over to the mirror which hung above the washstands. She stood wide-eyed, gaping at her reflection looking like a mummy wrapped in toilet paper, and didn't know whether to laugh or cry.

She fled through the hallways, ignoring all the insults, and finally arriving in the spare room, Miss Alexis's eyes widened, unbelievingly, viewing her conspicuous imposition.

"It's those girls! They did it, Miss Alexis. They said it was for you!" Gina panted raveling her tale of woe as Miss Alexis patiently tidied her; nothing like Fanny's mal-treatment, Gina thought, gratefully.

Miss Alexis tried reasoning with her that perhaps the girls were just letting off steam from being scolded the evening prior. It was Miss Alexis's nature to be understanding and Gina agreed, unwillingly.

As each day passed, Gina incurred a crisis of sorts, at the mercy of someone; whether it stemmed from broken dishes, to food, purposely spilt to the floor, she was lashed; in addition to Diane's lies and false accusations, causing her to be beaten. Her tell-tale bruises were evident and she was always a pathetic sight. Undoubtedly, Miss Alexis had come to accept her tale of the horrible goings-on.

Miss Alexis had threatened to reprimand everyone but Gina objected; pleading that she'd only be subjected to worse abuse. Miss Alexis heeded her plea, bowing down reluctantly.

One spring morning, Gina awoke with an annoying pain in the lower area of her back. Each day however, the pain worsened, and she was constantly walking around with her hand behind rubbingand soothing.

During a class session, Miss Alexis was tutoring about forms of etiquette and the importance of the words, "PLEASE" "MAY I" and "THANK YOU", in addition to, the importance of being truthful to one's self and to others when suddenly, a sharp pain attacked Gina. Her legs cramped and she moaned in pain as Miss Alexis massaged and comforted her.

"I noticed you rubbing your back often, dear. Have you had other attacks?" Miss Alexis asked.

"No! But I've had a bad pain back there for a long time! I was afraid to tell you."

"Never be frightened of me, dear! You report it to Miss Adler. She'll take care of you."

The pain slowly subsided and during lunch break, Gina scurried to the office. Miss Adler stared fixedly at her and spurted, "What do you want here, Miss Prissy?"

"I--I have a bad pain down here," Gina stuttered, pointing to the area. "It hurts bad, sometimes. I had it for a long time. Can you help me?"

"You have forgotten what I preach," she cracked Gina "slab-dab" across the face, shocking her, and she began to cry. "Your pain is imaginary! Something you have thought up to get attention. Do not bother me! Be off with you!"

Gina ran out flabbergasted. Miss Alexis was correct when she'd mentioned that Miss Adler would take care of her; but she didn't realize in which manner. Gina vowed never to tell her about the incident. It would only anger her and she'd want to talk with Miss Adler; and for being nosey, might send her away. Gina knew what spitefulness was all about and fibbed to Miss Alexis that all was okay!

The pain shadowed her, recurring frequently. She'd wondered how much longer she could continue pretending and tolerate all the horrible abuse.

Almost three weeks gone, during one night, Gina awakened crying in agony. She felt feverish. She placed her hand under herself and felt sopping wet. She'd wet the bed and in a frenzy, she would lay moaning in her wetness as the pain gradually lessened.

In the morning, the girls were busy changing their sheets. "Today is Friday!" she whispered relieved. "Miss Orr won't have to know!" Quickly, she changed into her clothes and hung her wet nightgown behind the dresser to dry. Hastily, she gathered up clean linen and rushed making up her bed; pain and all.

During class session, she felt dizzy. She was hurting when Miss Alexis said, "You don't look well, dear! Is something wrong?"

"It's that pain, Miss Alexis! It never went away! I lied!" Gina admitted, revealing the truth about Miss Adler and why she'd lied. "I'll go through anything as long as you're with me. I don't ever want to lose you! Not ever!"

Miss Alexis embraced her, mentioning that she'd had a few discussions with Miss Adler regarding clothing, illness, and everyone's nasty attitudes; and she'd been told not to meddle or Miss Adler would take drastic measures. "As a matter of fact, dear! I believe your supposition may be correct."

"I'm scared, Miss Alexis! I wet my bed and it's lucky today is Friday, the day to change bed sheets or I know I'd have been beaten badly."

"You did nothing terrible, dear. Sometimes, when a person is ailing or hurts as you do, it's likely to happen. Miss Adler and Miss Orr should realize that!"

Gina endured discomfort the remainder of that day and all through the night, and awakening that morning, she was wet and smelled awful. She was frantic and petrified to get out of bed.

It was just her bad luck that Miss Orr should enter the dormitory. She was clapping her hands to get the girls full attention and glanced in her direction. "You there? Why are you still in bed?" Miss Orr plodded over to her. "Get up out of that bed!" She pulled the covers off, tugging at her nightgown. "I see the problem! You wet the bed!" She smacked her.

"I don't know why it happened!" Gina cried.

Miss Orr struck her again, shouting, "I don't want to hear excuses!" She pulled her out of the bed, perching her on the edge of it. "You will sit there until I return! This is a matter for Miss Adler!" She stormed out.

She sat crying in pain and shivering. She was scared out of her wits.

"So, Little Orphan Annie peed her bed!" Diane's sickening voice piped up.

"She probably stinks like a skunk," Joyce giggled.

Some of the girls began skipping in front of her, holding their snoots, hollering, "She sure does stink! She smells like my doghouse at home! Pee-ewe!" They pretended to cough strenuously.

Shortly, Miss Adler charged into the dormitory, in leaping, giant steps, over to Gina. She pulled at her braids and stood her an her feet. "So, Miss Prissy wet her bed! Well, I will remedy that situation."

"I didn't mean to! Maybe it's the pain! It never really went away."' She was swatted in the mouth.

"Your manners, Miss Prissy! You and your pain! It gives me a pain!" She shoved her aside, carelessly pulling the wet sheet from the bed, folding it in half. "I'm going to punish you my way; a lesson you will never forget!" She looked towards the girls. "I need a safety pin."

"I have one," a girl responded, rushing to her nightstand to retrieve it, then rushed back. "Here's the pin."

"Thank you child. What is your name?"

"Janet," she replied.

"Well, thank you, Janet," she turned her attention to Gina, and squeezing at her shoulders, pulled her up close. She shook out the folded sheet from behind, allowing it to topple over Gina's head. She was trembling and falling apart within, as Miss Adler fastened the sheet with the pin under her chin. "Now, Miss Prissy! Get yourself out into that hallway and march! You will not rest until I think you have learned your lesson! Do you understand?" She lashed at her legs.

"Hah! She looks like a scary ghost," Janet harped, gaping with her smug brown eyes, and twirling her banana curls.

"Yeah! One who pees the bed too!" Joyce chuckled.

The girls emerged from out the dormitory on their way to the cafeteria, teasing, when Diane clamped her fat nose and said, "I can't bare the stink. Let's go! Bye, bye, "Ghost!" Don't get lonely!"

Barefooted she marched, and each step she took on the marble floor was shocking cold, adding to her awful pain and humiliation. Why couldn't Miss Adler understand? Gina didn't mean to wet the bed. Miss Alexis understood! Miss Adler is just plain mean. She hates Gina. Her thoughts rattled on and on, then deviated to Janet, and why she hadn't been smacked or scolded for not calling Miss Adler as she demands; and she does. Miss Adler was all sugar and spice to her and she growled at Gina.

Hours later, she was still parading, growing weaker and felt burning alive. Her pain was worsening. She wished that Miss Alexis were head of the school. Everything would be right then. She was tiring She wanted to sit and rest but was afraid Miss Adler would sneak up on her and catch her. Her tears wouldn't cease and her thoughts preyed on hate.

Suppertime had rolled around, and Gina was beaten to the ankles. She wondered if Miss Alexis knew what was happening to her. She was so hungry and thirsty. She had to go to the bathroom and felt going crazy.

By nightfall, she heard Miss Adler's clopping footsteps nearing. "I hope you will have learned a lesson today, Miss Prissy." She unfastened the pin, pulling the dried-out sheet roughly from Gina's head. "Make up your bed with this same sheet. You may go to the lavatory then go immediately to bed." She handed Gina the sheet, sticking the pin in her dress pocket.

Gina's eyes were swollen from weeping and she stumbled, feeling her way into the bathroom. She leaned over the washbasin, turned on the water tap and sipped until she thought, she'd burst.

In the morning, she awoke drenched and was overcome with fear, when she heard Diane chirp, "Did you pee the bed, skunk?"

Momentarily, Miss Adler appeared. Gina shook fiercely and felt to puke. "I came personally to see if you've learned your lesson, Miss Prissy." She pulled off the covers, feeling the sheet. "Just as I thought, you haven't learned a thing. Sit up!"

Gina rose slowly, hardly able to see out of her eyes, moaning, "The pain! It hurts bad!"

"You often forget your manners! Don't you?" Miss Adler slapped Gina's face. "Your pain is a pretense to get sympathy! It won't work with me." She wacked her again.

The identical punishment was rendered and only the Almighty could spare Gina strength. She walked and walked until her legs felt like they were going to fall off; they ached so bad. Her thoughts had become erratic, diverting from one extreme to the other. She was so thirsty. Her lips had parched and her mouth was burning inside. She was starving. Her pain was agonizing, limping with every step.

She faintly heard the footsteps nearing her and thought it was Miss Adler, sneaking up on her, when she heard, "Gina, dear!"

By the power and grace of the Almighty, her ears perked. Her eyes strained and lamely she fettered into Miss Alexis's angelic arms, sobbing hysterically, body and soul.

Miss Alexis squatted, propping Gina on her lap. "Oh, Gina, dear." she sighed sadly. "I hate to see what is being done to you. I'm so sorry! One day, the Almighty will show his power. Right will right itself and there will be penance to pay."

"It don't matter! You came! That's all that matters, Miss Alexis." Gina sniffled, and gently felt Miss Alexis's angelic face, her mouth, feeling tears shedding from her blue eyes. "I could hardly see you, Miss Alexis. I miss you so much and I love you a whole bunch too!" she rested her feeble body against Miss Alexis to indulge in her warmth.

"Gina, dear. I want to help you so much, but I'm like stuck in a corner. I've threatened Miss Adler, but I won't go into that now. I'm only worried about you, dear. I was told to stay away from you, but I went against Miss Adler's wishes. I had to see you, but now, I must sneak off just as quickly. Be strong, dear! I'll return. I love you dearly; You're my little girl. Always remember that."

Nine days of bed-wetting, excruciating pain, merciless punishment and near starvation, Gina's little body mentally and physically collapsed.

CHAPTER FIVE

Gina was trying effortlessly to open her eyes and was wriggling in pain, moaning. "Miss Alexis! Miss Alexis! Why don't you believe me? I hurt! I hurt badly! Please help me!" Gina cried deliriously.

In the midst of her moaning, she felt hands restraining her. "Where does it hurt, dear? I want to help you." Dr. Parson spoke concerned.

"It hurts here, Miss Alexis! Help me!"

"Doctor Parson!" Miss Alexis voiced. "The child thinks she's in school, the poor little thing. Gina told me that she had been badly abused; and that she's had a distressing pain in her lower back and wettingthe bed."

"Sounds like a kidney problem! We'll find out!" Dr. Parson remarked.

"She looks like she's gone through hell."

"Yes! It's a darn shame, but child abuse, particularly in a school, is difficult to prove. Suppose you give the child an injection to ease her pain and I'll be off. I'll need blood samples and a urine specimen in the morning."

"Gina. You're going to be okay. You're in a hospital and you can set your fears aside." She was doted a love tap. "I'm Miss Renz, a nurse, and I personally will be attending to your care." She pulled off the sheet, easily turning Gina on to her side. Gina felt a small area of her butt being rubbed and a sharp, piercing sensation engulfed her, causing her to cry. "It's all over, dear. In a little while you'll be feeling no pain.

Gina lay on her back sniffling and trying to force her eyes to open. Curiously, she placed both her hands to her eyes and felt with her fingers two huge, puffy mounds. They feel so big, she thought and strangely, her body began to tingle. She was feeling like a description she'd read about in a book, "floating on a cloud."

Unbelievingly, her pain was gone; just like magic, she thought, mentioning it to Miss Renz.

"It's the sting you felt, it had medicine in it! That's your magic. You'll be needing more of them along with other medications."

"I'm going to call it the "Magic Needle," and since I know it's going to help me, I won't cry!"

"Good idea!"

"Miss Renz, I wish I could see you, but thank you for taking such good care of me."

"You can thank Miss Alexis. She's the one who rushed you here into emergency and saw to it that you get special care and your own room. You'll be taken there shortly. She insisted the very best for you. She must love you very much."

"And I love her. She's been just like a mommy to me. She's my tutor, and teaches me lots of things. Miss Renz! I'm so thirsty. May I have some water, please? My mouth burns inside and the water makes it feel better."

"Let's have a look. Open your mouth wide." She examined. "My Lord! It's a bad case of canker sores; lack of food and vitamins is usually the cause; and from the looks of you; it's no wonder. You need fattening up; and medication each day will heal those sores." She poured a large glass of water.

Through a straw, Gina sipped the water, drinking excessively. "That was so good," she panted.

"Thank you, Miss Renz."

"Now, open your mouth real wide again." She dabbed a purple colored medication.

"It tickles funny." Gina gurgled.

Shortly, she was wheeled onto an elevator; and how her tummy tickled whenever it stopped at a floor level. When arriving in her own, special room, she was put into bed. Miss Renz placed moist patches over her eyes then she fell into a deep, long awaited, peaceful sleep.

Clanking sounds awakened her. She was stressed with pain, but worse yet, she was sopping wet and surely believed that Miss Renz would punish her.

"Gina, I have breakfast, but first those patches come off, then the magic needle."

Upon the patches being removed, Gina shaded her eyes from the light, then slightly squinting, peeped through them and said, "I can see you, Miss Renz! Not good, but I can see you. You've got pretty blue eyes, and your hair is reddish."

"Why, thank you, dear." Miss Renz voiced as she prepared to pull down the covers.

Frantically, Gina blurted, "Miss Renz, I wet the bed! I'm sorry! Are you going to punish me?"

"Certainly not! I expected it! Eventually as you recuperate You'll stop." She injected, then primed Gina for the day.

A delicious breakfast was set before Gina and she felt like a queen sitting on a throne; just like her favorite fairy tales, she thought; and wished the school was like the hospital; with no one to take her food or hassle her. Gina's mouth burned with every bite, but she was so hungry and at peace with herself, devoured it totally.

Miss Renz removed the tray, assisted in brushing Gina's teeth, then took blood samples and a urine specimen. "You're set, my dear! Now simply relax and I'll check on you later." Miss Renz ran herself to the laboratory.

The hospital functioned on a precise and ridged schedule; as did Miss Renz performing her duties cheerfully, and to perfection. Beyond the call of duty, she'd retain children's books from the hospital library for Gina to read each day.

Weather permitting, she'd set Gina in a wheelchair, nice and comfy, and they would meander to a little creek, just beyond the hospital grounds and watch the tadpoles swimming about in the water.

On one of those outings, they had encountered a shabbily dressed, aged man. He was toothless and had a stubbly, gray beard. He was wobbly on his feet, warbling at the top of his lungs, and appeared dancing the boogie-woogie.

"Miss Renz. Why is he doing that?" Gina asked impressed.

"He's what's known as a "down-and-outer." "A drunkard!" Miss Renz sighed, compassionately. "He's a person who drinks liquor; is probably a frequenter of saloons or bars and gets so fired up, boggling the mind. In other words, the stuff can make a person crazy."

"What's liquor?"

"It's a liquid alcoholic beverage. It's bitter tasting."

"Is it like the alcohol you rub on my butt before you inject me with the magic needle?"

"Heavens no, dear!" Miss Renz giggled. "The beverage is brewed or distilled in refineries. It appears, more and more, that the young adults are zealously taken with this liquor stuff. I guess it gives them a big-shot attitude, then they go hot-rodding in their cars and create havoc! Young and elderly, whatever the reason for consuming excess liquor, is pure and simple foolishness." She lectured. It seemed like she could talk about the subject forever; as if that drunkard had struck a nerve, causing her to recall a memory. "Don't take me wrong, dear; drinking to be sociable is one thing, but drinking, just for the sake of drinking is another. Always, remember it! Liquor! It's a killer!"

It was an extra special day for Gina when Miss Alexis, looking as radiant as always, had visited her. There were no words to express the joy they shared together; and the gratefulness, love and respect Gina held for her. Truly, she was Gina's salvation. She was real, warm and kind; and had lived up to all her sympathetic qualities.

To Gina's surprise, she'd gifted her with a lovely nightgown and a book:

DOROTHY AND THE WIZARD IN OZ.

She was elated. "Oh, thank you, Miss Alexis! It's beautiful! I never had a new nightgown before! Now the girls won't tease me at school anymorc. I hate going back! I know it'll be very soon. Must I go back?"

"Yes dear! You'll be returning for the last half of the semester. Summer vacation, at school, is about over as well!"

With loving hugs, Miss Alexis departed to venture in pursuance of carrying out her missionary work. Gina disliked having her leave, but fully understood her gentle nature of wanting to reach out and help others; as, she did for her. And yes. Gina knew, in her little heart, that Miss Alexis wasn't a figment of her imagination after all!

During her two months stay in the hospital, Gina had regained her strength; even gained weight. Her kidney disorder fared well; and mentally, she was back to being a happy-go-lucky, contented, little eight year old, but reluctant to return to that horrible school. Her only consolation was being with Miss Alexis.

She bid farewell to Miss Renz; in all appreciation and trusted that the "Magic Needle" makes lots of people feel better, like she.

Entering her room was Miss Jacobs. Gina was surprised to see her. She expected to see Miss Alexis. "I will be returning you to the boarding school." She said gruffly and snapping her long skinny fingers, Gina trailed behind, walking a rapid pace and thinking; Miss Jacobs is still Miss Jacobs, never a smile and always in a hurry.

Miss Jacobs opened the passenger door of her shiny, black car, and Gina squirmed herself onto the red, smooth velveteen covering of the seat.

As she drove at a steady pace, Gina would intermittently glance in her direction. She'd noticed that her brown frizzy hair had grayed and the thick lenses in her new granny glasses had intensified her icy brown eyes to a frightening degree. She dared to tell her about some of the horrible goings-on in the school, but Miss Jacobs never responded. She'd asked her why she'd put her in that crazy house and Miss Jacobs retorted with a vexatious look, that if looks could kill, Gina would be dead.

Gina's insides rumbled when the school came into view and at the thought of seeing everyone again. She'd hoped that maybe they'd all changed in their wicked ways.

As they entered the main building, Miss Adler was entering her office and spied them approaching her. "Well, Miss Prissy! I see you've returned!" She spoke sarcastically. "You'll remain in the same dormitory and occupy the same bed, since you so conveniently wet and stained it. You may go to the library. You'll find Miss Alexis there."

Gladly, she flew to the spare room and, catching her breath, called out, "Miss Alexis! Miss Alexis! Surprise! I'm back!"

Miss Alexis was pleased to see her and they shared hugs and innermost words. "No one mentioned you were returning today! I should have been notified! Tomorrow the second half of the semester resumes!"

"I wondered where you were? The social worker drove me here. She's an odd-ball! Never talks! She's scary too! I didn't forget my book or nightgown either!"

Gina noticed that Miss Alexis's mind was elsewhere, and that her face wore a puzzled expression when she voiced, "I'm disturbed. Why wasn't I informed you were returning today? I'd of enjoyed picking you up. We could have spent the entire day touring and dining out. I suppose Miss Adler might be behind it all." The comment shocked Gina. "I'm not sure, but I can surmise! Sit down, dear. We can talk a while, before lunchtime." She cupped Gina's hands. "Do you remember when you were ailing? I'd mentioned that I wanted to help you, but was stuck in a corner."

"Not really, Miss Alexis"

"Well, no matter! It was at that time that I'd threatened Miss Adler that I'd confer with the board of advisory, and she, not the least bit concerned, made it clear, that it's her word against mine. She had the audacity to acknowledge if there were problems the girls would back her up claiming to have had a free-for-all fist fight; and that would be the end of that. Can you imagine?" She grew angrier by the minute. "She'd warned me that if I intended to remain in the school, I'd better stay out of her business. I'd recalled your objectionable pleas and was caught in the middle."

"And you did right, Miss Alexis. I'd told you before, I'd go through anything rather than lose you. I love you a whole bunch! Did Miss Adler holler at you for taking me to the hospital?"

"Oh, gracious no! She'd only informed me that I'd made a wise decision; saving her from embarrassment. Oh, how those words had infuriated me! I blasted at her! I said something like; You abused and neglected the child till she was almost dead and have the gall to worry about embarrassment? I'd left in disgust; leaving her to examine her conscience. Now you can understand my assumptions!" The lunch bell rang. "Go have your lunch, dear, then return.

Gina was leery when entering the cafeteria, waiting last to be served. She walked over to the counter, wearing a happy-go-lucky smile, when Fanny said, "Well, if it isn't the orphan kid!" She slopped Gina's food that looked like gruel for animal feed.

Gina moseyed off thinking, Fanny hadn't changed a bit. She's still an old biddy, and a frown replaced Gina's smile. Some of the girls hopped out of their chairs and began shuffling behind her, sputtering unbecoming names, and fat Diane made a beeline for her food, sneaking off with her bread and pudding.

Gina's first day back, and they were picking on her. She was bitter. Food and all, she cleared her tray into the garbage can, then marched herself back to the spare room. She hated those girls. She hated Diane, most. She hated everyone, and thought why did she have to come back?

She caught Miss Alexis in the act of setting, on the counter, numerous colorful looking jars. "Those are watercolor paints! It was to be a surprise. You returned earlier than expected; and from the looks of you, lunch didn't go over too well. Feel up to painting?" She conned a smile from Gina's frowningface. Happily, they painted colorful pictures; getting more on themselves than on the paper. They were a colorful mess and having fun.

Gina tolerated a stormy supper of assorted cooked vegetables being flipped at her and of name calling. Diane must've had ants in her pants. She kept jumping out of her chair and rocking Gina's, shuffling her about; then, she'd release the chair and Gina would go flying forward into the edge of the table with a thud. Oh, how Gina wished she were back in the hospital. She consumed a bit of her food, and in a dither, left the cafeteria and prepared to bathe.

Recovering her nightgown, she treaded to the washroom. The tubs were situated in eight, partitioned little rooms. She utilized the first one, closing the door, but not locking it; recalling Miss Alexis's words. "Never lock the door! For practical purposes."

She ran the water then stepped into the tub, splashing, humming and washing. She was just about to step out of the tub, when Diane opened the door and was holding a large bucket in her hand. She squeezed through the door as each glared at one another scornfully then, quick as a wink, she poured ice cold water all over Gina, then scurried sideways out the door.

Shocking cold, Gina shrilled, "You fat tub of lard, Diane! You crazy idiot!" She sat her shivering body back into the warm water, observing the goose bumps as her teeth chattered.

Proud as a peacock, she ambled into the dormitory wearing her new nightgown which Diane was quick to notice. "Hey, dummies," she shrilled. "Little Orphan Annie is wearing a new nightgown and thinks she's in our ritzy bracket! Wishful thinking huh, Gina?"

Gina simply meandered on, withdrawing to bed.

CHAPTER SIX

Opening her eyes in the morning, impulsively, Gina felt her nightgown for wetness. She was powder dry and relieved. When stepping out of bed, her eyes focused on little, individual, colored pictures taped on her footlocker, nightstand, and walls.

She took a closer look. "Little Orphan Annie." She read the caption on one of the pictures. Viewing the others, she realized they were all of a comic strip and recalled the school ruling, peeling the pictures off when from behind she heard, "What is all this?" She looked over her shoulder and saw Miss Adler leering at her.

"I didn't put!" a stinging slap intervened.

"It is Miss Adler to you! I don't want any lip!" Her handy ruler came slashing down, catching Gina's wrist, and it began bleeding. "That was for disobeying rules." She neared her and Gina backed away. "Get over here!" Miss Adler screamed. She pulled on her nightgown, feeling it all over. "I see you didn't wet your bed. You did learn a lesson after all! I came to check on you personally! Your punishment did penetrate that empty head of yours. Now get all that nonsense down immediately."

Sniffling, she went to peeling the pictures off, bunching them, and wiping the oozing blood with it, when Diane sounded off. "Hey!

Little Orphan Annie! What did you think of yourself? It was our way to let you know how much we all missed you!" She badgered.

"Hey, Diane! We didn't bargain for all that now, did we?"

"Hell no!" Diane giggled.

"Couldn't have been better timing." Janet chimed in.

"And to think it was all my idea!" Joyce boasted. "I'd saved those comic pages quite a while. I'd planned reading them in my, so-called…bored moments!"

It sickened Gina, listening to them gloat. She wished she could pull every strand of hair out of their evil heads, and button-up their foul mouths.

In a huff, she tended her chores, then was bound for the spare room. Classes were resuming and she'd missed learning her reading, writing and arithmetic.

Miss Alexis had prepared assignments which kept Gina occupied and learning. Each day she'd take a step further, teaching her social studies and a bit of history. Gina enjoyed every subject, but she was still having a difficult time grasping English grammar.

It was during an afternoon session, when Gina had developed stomach cramps and anxiously called, "Miss Alexis! I have to go to the bathroom? May I please go now?"

"Go quickly then, dear." Miss Alexis said.

She sped out of the room holding her backside to restrain what could have been a messy situation. While sitting on the commode, some girls had tip-toed into the bathroom. "We're not supposed to be in here, so keep your voices low." It was Diane shushing the girls. "Okay, Joyce! Give us the low-down on all those cuss words your sister wrote you about, that can't be said in front of adults; it wouldn't matter here, though...not in this dive. Miss Orr is so dumb, she wouldn't care anyway. She knows which side her bread is buttered on; it's our folks who foot the bill and are always giving her and others real expensive gifts; and the mullah talks. I still wonder how the hell that orphan kid got into this joint; no folks; no money!"

"Yeah, we all wondered about that too!" Janet's voice piped up.

The situation was a chance in a-million, occurrence and hearing them talk about her, Gina sat scared and silent. She hoped that she wouldn't sneeze or ripple out a fart that would give her away.

"Okay! Let's get on with it, Joyce." Diane said.

"Okay! Well you all know shit!"

"Yeah! I know it as poop and cocky too!" a strange voice popped up.

"Okay! The next is, bitch! It's a word used in anger! It means lots of things! I don't know exactly!" She paused. "Well, another is bastard! It's supposedly what they call a baby that a girl has before she is married. It's a real bad thing! Now, let's get out of here! Tell you more later!" They shot out the door.

"Whew! Sure glad they're gone!" Gina uttered, tidying herself. She trotted back to the spare room, intending to tell Miss Alexis about the awful cuss words she'd overheard, but thought it wise to refrain.

Miss Alexis had left for the weekend; her customary mission obligation.

On the Saturday, before lunch, the girls were at the playground, and Gina thought to meander to the old abandoned house.

On her return, a girl, with slightly crossed, brown eyes and long, stringy black hair had purposely tripped her, causing her to bruise herself.

Gina was late getting to the cafeteria and Fanny had chewed her out with a vengeance.

"A girl tripped me outside, and I was washing off." Gina explained, pointing to her wounds.

"Means nothing to me, kid! You be here promptly or no eats."

Fanny crudely slid a tray of food across the counter. Gina studied it, then slightly grinned, thinking; Not much slopping she could do with split pea soup. She trampled off to settle in her chair.

"Hey, Tina! We nearly shit our guts out laughing when you tripped the skunk, watching her roll on the gravel." Joyce tittered.

"Oh, that! Little Orphan Annie got in my way! If you know what I mean!" Tina sniggered.

Gina slowly sidled her eyes to see who Tina was. "It was her who tripped me. The cross-eyed jerk." She muttered crossly.

"Hey skunk!" Diane winded. "I got my eye on that strawberry ice cream," she wiggled her fat fanny out of the chair, and snagged the back of Gina's head. As she grabbed for the ice cream, she shoved Gina's face smack-dab into the bowl of soup.

Stunned, she jerked her head up, in tears, and was slightly burning as she listened to all the dummies blustering corny jokes and laughing at her.

Miss Orr, fast as the dickens, froze in her tracks, goggling with those hideous eyes of hers then shouted, "So you want to be a clown, do you? See if this is funny!" She began lashing at her.

"She ought to wear that face all the time Miss Orr." Janet crowed. "It looks better than her own."

Weeping, and pea soup dripping, she fled to the bathroom. When eyeing herself in the mirror, she thought for sure, she was seeing a bull frog with only the whites of its eyes peeping through the green. That fatso, Diane! I hate her so much! I wish I were bigger than her, just for a little while! I'd pounce her into the ground but good." She began thinking about Miss Alexis theorizing; Be strong; Always keep hoping for a better day; Forgive your enemies; and she bouted with those words, trying to justify right from wrong.

Nearing Halloween, one evening, in the dormitory, the girls sat huddled, on the floor planning a Halloween party. "We don't have much time before Halloween comes, so listen up, dummies!" Diane Stressed. "Our parents will be visiting on the weekend. Ask them to bring a costume for yourselves, and a few apples stuffed with coins so we can dunk them."

"Don't forget the funny prize, Diane," Joyce reminded.

"Oh, yeah! Have your folks wrap a funny prize so we can exchange gifts."

"Will we play some games too?" A younger girl asked.

"We'll see, dummy!" Diane replied. "Oh, and another thing! Ask your parents to bring some goodies and something to drink. If I think of anything else I'll let you know."

"Sounds like we'll have lots of fun," Janet said.

"You know it!" Diane assured. "Hold it a minute! I got to ask something. Hey, skunk! You want to come to our party?" Gina's ears perked. "You won't even need a costume! You can come as you are! We'll even let you win first prize as the Ugly Duckling, and present you with mice turds!"

Gina fell back onto her pillow disappointed; just when Diane seemed sincere, in the same breath she cuts into her like a knife; and Diana knowing full well the invite was all a hoax.

From the first day Gina had returned from the hospital, she had deferred to a rough road of torment and abuse. Her class sessions were her only blissful moments. Miss Alexis kept Gina "on her toes." She was having fun learning. Like the day she said, "Gina, would you like to play in the gymnasium?"

"Oh, I would, but there's no one to play with me." Gina replied.

"I will!" Miss Alexis chuckled. "I'm not so old that I can't still get around. I'll teach you how to play badminton."

"You will! You're not ashamed to play with me?"

"Of course not! Let's go!" They strutted off.

It hadn't taken Gina long to attain the knack of holding and swinging the racquet properly. She was a little tyke, but she sure had a mean swing. "This is fun, Miss Alexis!"

"I'm enjoying myself too, dear, but I think I'll rest on the bench for a while."

"Miss Alexis, while you're resting, may I go play on the mat?"

"Go ahead, dear. I'll watch from here."

She stood on the cushioned mat imitating Diane, trying to touch her toes. "I'm doing it, Miss Alexis! I'm touching my toes!"

Before they knew it the dismissal bell sounded and classes were over for the day. They were having such a great time and reluctantly they left. "They'll be plenty of other days, dear. I'll see to that," Miss Alexis said cheerfully.

A change of season, and the weather was becoming colder and Gina, to retreat from her merry-go-round of abuse, strolled one last time to the spacious fields and meadows, remembering when Miss Alexis would take her frolicking merrily, and picking wild flowers. When Miss Alexis would tire, a log or a huge rock became her resting post. She'd softly recite nursery rhymes or hum child limericks, then Gina would lovingly curl up flush against her, humming along.

She'd recalled all the books she'd read on the steps of the old abandoned house and one in particular came into mind titled: WHITE SATAN which related to a beautiful white horse who'd been badly mistreated and harassed daily by its master. One day, the horse could no longer take the hurt and fled to other pastures. Oh, how Gina felt like that horse, but at least the horse was free to roam, she'd thought. Where would she go? Who'd want a scrawny, freckle nosed, looking orphan?

Time was whizzing by. Thanksgiving Day had come and gone, and already, Christmas had swooped in. The girls had left for the Christmas and New Year holidays. Gina welcomed the breather and freedom from hostility, but grieved wishing she had a mommy and daddy to go home to.

Miss Alexis was preparing to voyage tending her missionary work, but before departing, she gifted Gina with an exquisite gold cross and chain.

"It's so pretty! Thank you, Miss Alexis! I will always treasure it just like my little trinkets."

"Trinkets?"

Gina quickly recovered them within a dresser drawer. "See!"

"They are exceptional! Why two sets?"

"I'd lost the first set that my lady friend Annie who used to visit me at the foster homes I'd lived in, gave me. I never knew who she really was, but she was kind; just like you. One day, she never returned. I don't know why! I loved her lots; just like I do you. When she'd learned that I lost the trinkets she'd brought me another set. I found the original and was left with two sets."

"Do you know what each represents?"' Miss Alexis asked.

"No!" Gina said anxiously awaiting her response.

"Well, dear. The anchor represents hope! The cross symbolizes faith, and the heart realizes charity. And Gina, if you ever chance to believe in something strongly; and if held infinitely within your heart can bring about joyous miracles.

Together they bid their heartfelt ado's then Miss Alexis darted off.

Miss Adler must have worn the soles of her shoes out seeking Gina, and when she found her, saw to it that she would not be loafing around, assigning her a workload of chores.

The entire two weeks, she had placed herself in a world of fantasy. She pretended to be Cinderella as she scrubbed, mopped, polished; in addition to cleaning the inside of windows. She professed Miss Adler as the intolerable stepmother, Diane and her dummy pals were the obnoxious stepsisters, and Miss Alexis was her fairy godmother.

The chores had been exhausting yet challenging. She had just finished tidying up the kitchen and was returning to the dormitory when she heard uproarious laughter and gabbing.

"Those dummies are back," she murmured unhappily, and upon entering the dormitory, she saw piles of luggage and junk on the beds and everywhere. Unnoticed, she took refuge in her bed.

CHAPTER SEVEN

Gina opened her sleepy eyes and heard what sounded like a choir moderately singing; must be a radio, she thought, lazily stepping out of bed. Casually, she glanced towards the girls, noticing it was they who were harmonizing; golly gee, what got into them, she wondered?

She quickly tended her chores then headed for the spare room hoping that Miss Alexis had returned for the start of the third semester. Since she hadn't, she promenaded to the cafeteria.

She sensed the girls were all too calm and evasive, particularly blabbermouth, Diane. Unexpectedly, she saw Tina dash past her from the opposite side of the table. She confronted Miss Orr looking as if she'd been crying, and catching her breath, excitedly exclaimed that someone had stolen her ring.

She insisted that she'd placed it on her nightstand, and realizing she'd forgotten it returned to fetch it and it was gone.

Miss Orr's eyeballs seemed spinning in eagerness as she quizzed the girls; and they all swore up and down, that they'd seen Tina place the ring on her nightstand.

In the midst of all the commotion, Miss Orr questioned Tina if she or anyone had left the dormitory before leaving for the cafeteria; and if so, who remained behind?

"A bunch of us girls had gone into the bathroom. I don't recall who stayed behind exactly, but I sure can tell you, that orphan kid wasn't with us." Tina spurted.

"That's it!" Miss Orr said tapping her forehead as if to dislodge her cluttered thoughts, trudging over to Gina. "So you're the thief!"

She drew her own conclusions. "Miss Adler shall hear about this!" She gritted at her buck teeth and fled.

"She believed me! She believed me!" Tina broke into stitches laughing.

"Wait till Miss Adler finds out! Wow! They'll sure be some fireworks!" Diane laughed into her sleeve. "I knew the minute Tina mentioned the skunk, Miss Orr would get all wound up and accuse her. I thought for sure, she'd want to look through her stuff for it. I got a feeling Miss Adler will though."

"Tina! You make a terrific actress," Joyce praised. "Miss Orr sure fell for your chicken shit story. Where'd you hide the ring?"

"Oh! In an easy enough place to find. That's if Miss Adler decides to look for it. We don't know that yet! But so far, everything is going "okeydokey" as planned." Tina raved.

Worrisomely, Gina bowed her head. She was scared and wishing she could run away. Like clockwork, the gabbing silenced and her heart began to thump. Suddenly, she felt her ears being pulled and twisted, and she was dragged out of her chair. She was in agony, screaming, "What did I do?

I didn't do what you think I did!" she held fast to her aching ears.

"You forgot your manners, Miss Prissy," Miss Adler wacked her cheek. "Look at me when I speak," she jerked Gina's head back. "Why did you steal Tina's ring?"

"I didn't! Honest, I didn't! I was in the library." She was wacked on the other cheek.

"Excuses! I don't want to hear them. Let's both march to the dormitory. I want to do a bit of searching." Her face began to flush. "If I find the ring amongst your belongings, you'll be punished severely."

Shaky and tearful, she paced behind Miss Adler and heard those evil devils in disguise meekly giggling and snickering, hinting their delightful triumph; and she wished she had a pitch fork to jab in their butts.

Gina's little legs wobbled so that she could hardly stand on her feet as she watched Miss Adler probe the inner and outer sections of the dresser drawers. In a fury, she attacked the bed, pulling the covers and all off. Suddenly, with brute force, she picked up the mattress, flinging it, and it settled upright against the wall. "So far, so good," she growled panting then charged towards the footlocker, checking the pockets or Gina's jacket and the top shelving. Kneeling herself, she examined the bottom of the locker, scraping corners. "Ah, just as I thought!" She grunted to her feet, displaying the ring.

Gina panicked seeing the wickedness in her face. Those eyebrows of hers began twitching a mile a minute, and her fiery eyes could've burnt a hole through her when she said, "So you didn't take the ring, huh? You habitual, fiendish liar!" She put it in her dress pocket and then, in a whisk lunged for her shaking and jerking the living daylights out of her. She thrust her up against the dresser and quickly unfastened her handy ruler.

"Please, don't hit me!" Gina pleaded. "I swear I didn't do it!"

"You wretched liar! Liar! Liar! Habitual liar!" She shrilled like a mad woman, striking the ruler in accordance.

"Don't hit me no more! Please, no more!" Gina slipped to the floor and tried to edge herself away when she felt the sharp tip of the ruler slash between her shoulder blades, taking her breath away. She heard the ruler crash to the floor and quickly Miss Adler reeled her, face up, and began clouting her with beastly and crushing punches. She was like a crazy lunatic and out of her mind.

Abruptly, the pouncing ceased. Gina was trickling blood, and Miss Adler, breathing heavily blurted, "Now, Miss Prissy your aches and pains will be a reminder of what I do to a thief and a habitual, wretched liar." She picked up her ruler. "You will not leave the dormitory today except to go to the lavatory. Class or no class." She left in a huff.

Weak and dazed, she lay sobbing, despairingly thinking of Miss Alexis's words of wisdom clashing within her mind. She attempted to pick herself up but felt woozy and nauseous and as she stared at her bed in shambles, it triggered more tears to fall.

"Gina, are you here?" Miss Alexis called, spying her on the floor. "Gina. Dear! What happened here?" She threw some bags aside, kneeling beside her. "You're face! You're eyes! You're bruised and swollen everywhere!" She pecked at her wounds with her handkerchief. "Those nasty girls! What was in their minds to do this?"

"It wasn't the girls, Miss Alexis." Gina sniffled. "I mean part of it was them and the other was Miss Adler." She related the ordeal. "I didn't take the ring! You taught me never to steal and I wouldn't; somebody put it there so I would get a whipping; and I can't go to class today either."

"It is the reason I'm here. You weren't in class and I wondered where you were; perhaps ill or something?"

"Oh. Miss Alexis! Why does Miss Adler do the things she does? I just don't understand her way of thinking."

"One day, that awful woman will repent!" Miss Alexis looked upward towards the heavens as if wishing the Almighty would hear her. "What she's done today and in the past, righteousness will pave its way."

Gina's tummy was churning. She was holding down what wanted to come up, and although tottering her way to the bathroom, she arrived in the "nick of time" puking. In a while, she waddled to the washstand and gaped in the mirror, which reflected a pathetic massiveness of blood and swollen impressions everywhere. She moistened paper towels, and dabbed her wounds, shuddering and cringing from its sting.

She retraced her steps and found Miss Alexis had made up her bed. "Thank you, Miss Alexis! It's just like Humpty Dumpty, in a way, but you put it together! Oh, Miss Alexis! What would I do if I didn'thave you? Oh, I still feel funny. May I lay down?"

"First, I'll help you take off that stained dress, and you can get into your nightgown since you are not permitted in class today. You may as well be comfortable. I brought you a surprise! Something you have great need of." She set two, huge shopping bags, loaded to the hilt, on the bed. She fumbled in one of them and pulled out a pretty dress. "There is clothing in both bags for you. I hope they will fit."

"Clothing, for me! All for me!" Gina glowed overall and began to browse. "Miss Alexis, look! A pair of shoes and fluffy slippers; and look, a bunch of undies and a warm coat for winter." Gina excitedly pulled out mittens, a hat, dozens of socks, a few nightgowns, and last, numerous dresses. "Oh, Miss Alexis! It's all so nice. I never had much clothing; nothing of anything. I'm a lucky girl to have you. I love you so much." She gleefully embraced her then laid down to nap.

Gina slept beyond expected, awakening the following morning. Sleepily, she noticed the girls making up their beds. She was bewildered and wondered what happened to yesterday?

Aching everywhere, she slowly dressed, putting on one of the dresses that Miss Alexis had brought for her. It fit to a tea. She felt so proud; no more short dresses for her.

While making up her bed, she felt the floor tremor when nosey Diane trampled over to her. In her usual manner, she hushed the girls, wheeled Gina around to face them and said,

"Meet Miss Panda Bear!" She cheered and the dummies hurrahed along. "Boy, oh, boy! Look at those two terrific shiners! That's what you get for copping stuff. Miss Adler sure did a number on you!" She whistled herself away as the dummies laughed relentlessly.

Gina sped to the bathroom and fixedly stared into the mirror. Flashing back at her were two, large black circles around her eyes; the likeness of a panda bear with a nose as big as a walnut.

In dismay, she ran to the spare room and Miss Alexis gawked, like she was seeing things. Her eyes widened and they appeared horrified. "What did that woman do?" She was irked. "I wish I had a quick remedy to rid those black eyes, dear! In time they'll disappear."

"Diane said I look like a panda bear."

"Ignore her. One day, she'll get what's due her." Gina felt they were words to pacify. "Always remember, dear! The Almighty works in mysterious ways. And, by the way! You were sleeping sopeacefully last evening when I checked on you---I didn't want to disturb you."

Every spare moment, Gina's nose was ground into the pages of books and assignments. Learning was of the essence, and Miss Alexis was proud of her progress. Diane and her puppets carried on with their evil charades, and Gina weathered her wounds within; but her scars remain a constant reminder of the hate she bore.

Mid-February took its toll in illness. The dormitory resembled a hospital ward and smelled solely of medicated fumes escaping from several vaporizers. Gina had contracted, what Miss Alexis called, the intestinal grip and a stubborn chest cold. Miss Alexis kept a vigil watch over her; serving her dosages of putrid tasting medicines.

Diane, her clan, and several other girls were afflicted with laryngitis. Gina was tickled pink.

Her diarrhea, had grabbed hold, as it had in the last previous days, and she streaked to the latrine. Soon after, someone entered, occupying one of the partitioned toilets.

"Gina! She heard a voice call (surprised to hear her name). "I know it's you in there! I followed you. I have to be quick! I have a note for you," the girl whispered.

"Whoever you are, how come you're talking to me? I suppose the note is from fat Diane since she can't use her voice and is using you to do her dirty work." She jumped off the bowl to stomp on a cockroach.

"Oh, no! Honest! I've waited a long time to get you alone. You know... away from Diane and everybody. Diane would bust my head if she knew I was talking to you." Her voice quivered. "I just want you to know that I feel awfully sorry for you! I mean-- watching you get beat and all. Well it's all in the note. After you read it, tear it up and flush it down the bowl. Okay? It'll be our secret." She flung the note beneath the partition, leaving hastily.

As she commenced to read, she noted that the penmanship was clear and readable.

Gina. I remembered your name from the first day you came to this school, and I liked you right away. I wanted to make friends, but Diane stopped it. She's very cruel and mean. She acts big because she's so fat that everybody is scared of her. Me too! When she'd warned everybody to stay away from you, I did because she'd said she'd hit anyone who came near you. Her best dummy friends, Joyce, Janet, and Tina are mean too. I hate them for the lies they tell and twist around, then blame you for everything,and then, you get beat with that stupid ruler or something. I don't like Miss Adler or Miss Orr because they hit you all the time and never believe you when you try to tell them the real truth about everything. They're just as mean as Diane. I hate that Fanny too, and what she does to your food. Yucky! I want you to know that I don't laugh along with Diane anymore. I only fake it because I'm afraid of her. Also,I want you to know that I really do like you. You'd probably be a terrific friend. I want you to know that you do have a secretive friend "Me" even though you'll never know who I am or what I look like.A long time has passed, and I have held on to this note long enough. I just had to let you know how I feel. I'm so sorry to have to see you suffer so much. I like Miss Alexis, and I'm sure glad you have her to look after you.

Your friend, Ellen (a past dummy)

Tears rushed to her eyes wishing she knew who Ellen was, but it pleased her to know that she did, after all, have a friend who liked her. She was about ready to tear the note as Ellen had asked, but she was so impressed with it, and a thought told her to keep it. Folding it, she stuck it under the inside padding of her shoe. She returned to the dormitory, and unsuspecting, tried to seek Ellen out, but it was effortless.

Classes had been canceled for two weeks in hopes that everyone would've fully recovered. Miss Alexis prided herself at Gina's absolute recovery.

Her blackened eyes had disappeared and her swollen nose was back to normal proportion.

Diane was her usual nasty self, and the dummies lapped her behind.

The winter months had dwindled to the glorious spring. The trees were blossoming and the grass was turning an emerald green. Tulips and daffodils were blooming colorfully, in addition to the clustered lilac, which emitted its sweet fragrance.

The warm bright sun and freshness in the air captivated Gina's being, making her a helpless victim to spring anew.

CHAPTER EIGHT

Easter Sunday, a miraculous day that stirs the world each spring was ever present. Gina sat on her bed brooding, as in past years, watching the girls dress in their showy clothes. Oh, how they balked ungratefully about everything their parents had bought for them; each with their own complaint, griping about a dumb pair of black and white saddle shoes; or the shitty brown colored dress that flared out like a parasol; and some about their pocketbooks that looked like giant size school bags.

Oh, it truly irked Gina hearing those ingrates bullying their parents. They took so much for granted and she wondered what they would do if they didn't have no mommy or daddy, as she. Would they be squawking then, she thought? Impromptu, Ellen popped into her head. She felt sure that she appreciated her parents. She wished she knew who she was. She wanted to wish her a Happy Easter, but that was wishing the impossible.

Everyone left for the auditorium to meet with their parents when Miss Alexis entered the dormitory and said, "Gina, will you take a little walk with me?" She held out her hand for her to grasp. She guided her out of the building and into the faculty's dwelling, into her room. She sat on her bed, spilling several boxes which were propped one on top of another. "Clumsy me!" She grinned, adjusting them. "Come sit by me, dear. I want you to close your pretty eyes and don't open them until I tell you to."

She shut her eyes extra tight that she could see tiny white dots floating against a dark background. She heard paper crackling; and when given the okay to open her eyes, she gazed upon an exquisite, lavender and white, organdy dress. "Oh, it's so pretty!" Gina gasped.

"It's especially for you, dear; A very happy Easter."

Tears of joy swelled her eyes. She'd never owned a brand new dress before and she became emotional, thanking her. Miss Alexis vowed no tears and sorting through some of the other boxes, she showed a ruffled petticoat and undies, lavender socks, and a lavender ribbon for her hair. Gina was so excited when Miss Alexis completed the outfit, showing a black pair of dainty leather shoes and a small purse to match.

"Everything is so beautiful, Miss Alexis." Gina sniffled. "I'm just a little girl, but I understand lots of things, like if you weren't around to care and love me; you know what I mean, don't you?" She cuddled into her arms.

"I know very well, dear," she wiped a tear from her eye. "I can recall when I was a youngster. I was lonely just as you are. I grew up hoping that someone would love me. Oh, what am I saying! Today isn't the day to remember sad memories! Let's get you dressed and prettied up."

"How did you know my sizes, Miss Alexis?"

"Hah! That's my secret."

Miss Alexis had put the last finishing touches when Gina twirled over to the rectangular mirror that was secured on the closet door. Gleefully, she whirled, round and round, admiring her reflection.

"Look at me, Miss Alexis! I'm all brand new." She looked so elegant and her long, brown hair which extended beyond her little waist, flowed in soft waves.

Miss Alexis was gratified just looking at Gina, and swore She'd sprang from out a page of a child's fashion catalogue. She felt proud and was anxious to show her off to her foes.

Hand in hand, they headed for the auditorium. "Give them gals an eyeful, dear, but don't tell them a thing. Keep them guessing." Miss Alexis commented, leaving Gina on her own.

In all her splendor, she pranced into the auditorium. Those girls took one look at her and went "gaga," staring wide-eyed with their mouths hung open, in wonderment and surprise.

Diane caught a glimpse of her and hurriedly waddled over. She was garbed in a gaudy, chartreuse colored dress that fared out, saucer-shaped, from her waist. It looked like she was fermenting in a bulging, wine barrel as she glared, looking like the devil himself, digesting Gina's delicate loveliness. She was steaming and virtually took offense that she wasn't "top dog" and that Gina was nipping at her toes and busting a gut. She threw a fit insisting on learning where Gina had come by her finery.

Gina merely snubbed her, yet realizing that Diane would get her revenge, but this was her day and she was living it to the fullest.

Miss Alexis sought her out of the crowd and led her to the candy concession stand. "Pick out anything you like, dear," Miss Alexis said.

"Do you really mean it, Miss Alexis?"

Miss Alexis nodded and she became aware that her wishful thining's were coming true.

"Gina! Would you like to take a drive through the countryside and dine out?" Miss Alexis spoke loudly for all to hear.

"Can we?"

"When everyone has gone."

Late in the afternoon, they hopped in Miss Alexis's car. As they drove off, Gina's eyes wandered far and wide, capturing everything in sight. At the edge of a little town, they stopped at railroad tracks to allow a train to pass. Gina counted forty-seven cars which were loaded with coal and stuff. "Miss Alexis, what kind of a car is that yellowish, funny-looking last one?"

"It is called a caboose. It is generally used for the railroad workers and crewmen to relax, or whatever."

They drove on, resting at a picnic site equipped with swings and slides. Merrily, Gina swung on the swing that she'd always yearned to do. She felt like she was touching the sky when Miss Alexis pushed the swing, taking her higher and higher, tickling her tummy. She was happy as a lark and wished every day was like this day.

After Gina had had her fill, they drove on and wound up in the parking lot of an exclusive looking building that had huge wide bay windows and bright red drapes. "We'll dine in this restaurant." Miss Alexis acknowledged, and together they dined, enjoying the scrumptious cuisine.

Reluctantly, they journeyed back to the school. Miss Alexis escorted Gina to the dormitory. "I see none of the girls have returned," Miss Alexis said, helping Gina ready for bed.

"Miss Alexis, thank you for making this day a happy, happy one. I'll never forget all the nice things you've done for me. I love you so much."

"My day was just as pleasurable, dear! Watching you enjoy yourself was my delight. Goodnight, dear!" She kissed her forehead, dashing off and Gina fell asleep blissfully content.

In the morning, as Gina was gathering up her clothes to wear for the day, tubby Diane scuffled over to her. She roughly grabbed the front of her nightgown, and ruffling it tightly, lifted her on her tip-toes then said, "Okay, smarty pants! Who the hell did you think you were yesterday, Shirley Temple?" She joggled her and Gina kept tight lipped. "So, you won't talk, huh?" She released Gina then threw a mean punch to her chest. Gina keeled over, holding herself and hobbled to her bed, restraining her tears. "That ought to teach you not to get snooty with me." And oh, how Gina wished she was one of those mean old dragons that spurt hot flames of fire from their mouths. She'd rid herself of that phony for good.

The month of May had set in, and one day, during class session, Miss Alexis said, "Gina, do you know what day it is today?"

"No, Miss Alexis."

"Today is the first Friday in May. It's celebrated as Arbor Day; a special day appointed by law for pupils to plant greenery and create interest to protect forestry."

"I like plants and trees. I wouldn't hurt them."

"I'm sure you wouldn't, but others may." She picked up a package off the floor. "In this bag I have flower seeds and two small rosebushes. I thought it might cheer you up to watch something grow that you planted yourself."

Together, they carted all the necessary equipment outdoors, choosing a likely spot to plant. "How long do seeds take to sprout? And how often do I water them?" Gina questioned.

"Water them in reason to the weather and they should sprout within a few weeks."

Every day, rain or shine, Gina strolled to her little flower garden The rosebushes had rooted and new shoots had grown. After three weeks, the flowers had sprouted. She was thrilled.

"It's another miracle of the Almighty," Miss Alexis had reminded. "Next step is to pull out all the weeds."

Summer recess had rolled around. Bright and early, some of the girls were packing their duds to leave for summer vacation. Gina had no intention of hanging around to listen to those dummies hoot and holler their farewells, and chose to ramble to her garden of colorful flowers.

She picked a bouquet tor Miss Alexis and presented them to her. She was delighted with them, admiring their beauty while sniffing its sweet fragrances. They chatted awhile then Miss Alexis mentioned that she was preparing to leave shortly to continue her missionary work. She'd be returning when school resumed. Gina was heartbroken. Miss Alexis gifted her several paper doll cutout books along with a small pair of scissors. They bid their fondest farewells, but Gina hated leaving her.

Most or her day was spent sulking and cutting out paper dolls. When she tired, she hid her cutouts under the porch steps of the old abandoned house and skipped to her flower garden.

"My pretty flowers! My rosebushes!" she stared unbelievingly. "Someone pulled out all my plants!" she cried, falling to her knees. "They stomped and crushed them!" Heartbroken, she picked up the wilted petals.

"What'cha cry 'in about, little girl?" A strange, deep voice sounded from behind, startling her. Wiping her tears; she whipped around and saw an elderly man with silver, white hair and a little mustache peering down at her. "My garden! Someone pulled out all the flowers and rosebushes," she sniffled. "Did you do it, mister?"

"Not me, child! I take care of plants, not destroy them," he replied. "I'm Mr. Holden, the new caretaker."

"Caretaker? What's that?"

"You know! Mow 'in the grass, snipp'in bushes, and all that."

"I'm sorry I blamed you, Mr. Holden. It's just that my plants meant so much to me."

"I understand child. I did see a few girls hang 'in around here earlier. One was a mighty big one."

"That had to be Diane. She's a mean one too!"

"What'cha name, child?"

"Gina."

"A mighty pretty name for a mighty pretty little gal." He squatted beside her. "Look over yonder, Gina. I've set out several bird baths and filled them with water. Why don't ya' come here each day and watch the birds bathe? They sure are fun to watch. I'll bring ya' some bird seed so you can feed them. I'll bet'cha in a few days ya' make some fine feathered friends."

"You'll do that for me? I mean bring the bird feed?" Gina said questioning.

"Cross my heart! Tomorrow be here after lunch."

"Thank you, Mr. Holden. You're a kind man. I feel much better now. See You!"

She was so taken by Mr. Holden that the remainder of the day and all through the evening she couldn't think of anything but the bird baths and feeding them.

To pass the time away, she sat on her bed, reading the book Miss Alexis had gifted her when Diane spouted, "Hey, Mary, Mary, quite contrary; How does your garden grow? Have you watered your flowers lately, skunk? Crazy, but I thought the garden was a weed patch so I pulled everything out."Oh how Gina boiled and she went to bed.

During breakfast, unexpectedly, Miss Orr neared Gina and began lashing at her. "What did I do? What did I do?" She cried.

"You destroyed Diane's plants." She told me how you deliberately pulled the flowers out of the ground! You miserable child." She lashed her again.

"They were my plants! Me and Miss Alexis planted them. Diane lied! She pulled them out."

"Enough of your lies!" She slapped Gina's face. "Leave your tray and get out of my sight immediately!"

Gina scrambled outdoors towards her little garden and lay sobbing; wishing the school would burn down or something when she fell asleep.

A gentle tap on her shoulder awakened her. "Gina!" Mr. Holden called. "Are ya' okay? Ya' were sleep 'in, and I don't want'cha burn 'in in that hot sun." He shaded his warm brown eyes. "C'mon, get awake! It's sunny here."

"Do you have the bird feed, Mr. Holden?"

"Sure do!"

They were bound for the bird baths. Their presence scared the birds and they flew up in the trees. Mr. Holden assured Gina not to discourage; and that in time, those birds might be eating out or her hands.

Gina sat patiently watching the birds fly over the bird baths, flapping their wings and seemingly splashing each other. Soon they flew to the ground. She scattered some feed and they flew away again. "When they get use to ya', they'll stick around. You'll see."

Daily, Gina visited with the birds. Diane had kept her distance aware that Mr. Holden was nearby. At times, he was busy with his chores, and he'd set a bag of bird feed beside a particular tree for Gina.

Several weeks passed and the birds didn't scare anymore. Gina enjoyed watching the baby birds flock around the bird baths, briskly splashing and spraying themselves. They'd chirp, fuss and feud in their birdlike fashion, then they'd swarm at her feet for food.

The realization of having befriended the birds elated Gina, and through the entire summer, they entertained her. On stormy days, she would gaze out a window hoping to catch a glimpse of them, but their location was too far to sight them.

It was the evening before the end of the summer break. The girls were restless and complaining about the sweltering heat. Gina was brushing her hair when Diane expelled a grossly loud belch then said, "Hey, hag! Why the hell don't you cut off that mop? It makes me sweat just looking at it."

"Why don't you chop it off for her, Diane?" Joyce egged her on.

"Yeah! Great idea, I will." Diane hopped on her bed, retrieving a pair of scissors.

Gina didn't take them seriously until Diane strutted toward her and Joyce trailing. She backed away, wide-eyed and scared. Diane bunched Gina's hair. Gina begged, screaming to leave her alone, but those monsters wouldn't bug off.

"Here's the scissors, Joyce. I'll hold her while you cut."

Gina fought like a champ, but Diane overpowered her, forcing her to the floor. Diane quickly straddled her fat blubber atop of Gina and she felt crushed, gasping and gulping for air. Joyce cut away. "A little more, Joyce. You didn't cut nothing." Diane hollered.

"No more...please!" Gina wailed. "No more ..."

"Shut up, you crock of shit!" Diane scoffed. "Oh, Joyce, give me the scissors. I'll show you how to cut a mop," she snipped and snipped, throwing the hair in Gina's face. "There, all done." She groaned to her feet. "Boy, that buzzard gave me a hard time, but I'll feel lots cooler now."

"Holly-golly! That was a humdinger, Diane!" Joyce chuckled. as they merrily bobbed away, laughing along with the dummies.

Gina lay weeping pitifully, staring at her hair piled in a heap. She was out of her mind as she unsteadily picked up the hair and flung it into the bottom drawer of her dresser. She crawled into bed, crying herself to sleep.

Came morning, the touch of her unruly hair brought undying tears. The girls went hog-wild teasing and laughing at her.

"Looks as if she stuck her finger in a light socket; the way it sticks out all over," Tina giggled stupidly.

Gina couldn't stand listening to the jabber any longer. She dressed, made up her bed, then sped to her place of refuge--the bathroom; where else could she go? Miss Alexis wasn't around to comfort her. She stared into the mirror shocked. Tears fell from her eyes seeing her, once long hair, almost cut to her ears, and sticking out every which way, was gone. She felt sick. She wondered what Miss Alexis will think when she ganders at her looking like one of those shaggy dogs.

At breakfast, Fanny took one look at Gina's hair and rampaged into a fit of hysteria. "I see you did scalp yourself. I thought them gals were joshing me."

Gina asserted that she didn't cut her own hair, but Fanny only tuttted, then handed her a platter of food that looked like a mixture of soggy stew.

When Miss Orr eyed Gina, she blew her top! Her protruding eyeballs looked ready to propel right out of their sockets. "Incredible!" she squealed. "Incredible! You brazen child. What right did you have to cut your hair for?" She wacked her repeatedly.

"I didn't! I wouldn't!" Gina cried.

"You lie!" She struck a racking blow to her face. "Leave this premises now!" She swatted her again and again.

Gina ran in bitter tears, wishing she could leave this hell-hole, and in her frustration, thought to visit the birds. She knew at least they wouldn't mind having her around. Unknowingly, her fine feathered friends helped save her sanity.

From a distance, she sighted Mr. Holden opening the high, black, iron gate and spotted Miss Alexis's tan car driving in. In her excitement, she forgot about her hair. She ran as fast as her little feet would carry her to meet Miss Alexis in a bear hug embrace.

Miss Alexis noticed Gina had been crying; her eyes were red and freshly made bruises were evident. However, she didn't mention a word about it; She knew better than to ask.

They sat on the cool green grass, and Gina gabbed and gabbed about Mr. Holden's bird baths, feeding the birds with feed and how much she enjoyed the cutouts. The shocker was yet to come.

She fiddled about relentlessly trying to get up enough courage to tell her about her hair. She thought she must have noticed it by now. Several times she was ready to blurt it out, but it wouldn't come out, but when it did…Miss Alexis boiled. She was madder than a wet hen!

"I can't believe it! I just can't believe it! I'd noticed your hair looking awfully shabby. I thought perhaps your braids had gotten stuck inside your dress collar. I never, never would have surmised. Those girls have gotten too big for their own britches. I'd love to turn them over my knee and tan their hides!" She kept shaking her head, lost in thought.

"It's alright now, Miss Alexis." Gina patted her hands. "In another six months I'll be leaving this horrible place, and I hope I never have to see it again; but I'll miss you terribly, Miss Alexis."

Miss Alexis led Gina to her room. She tapered her hair, looking super in a short barb then cleansed her bruises.

Throughout the day, the girls spouted smutty remarks, but she ignored them all. Came nightfall, everyone retired early to bed to awaken refreshed, enabling them to welcome back the vacationers.

CHAPTER NINE

Classes began in full swing, and Miss Alexis's assignments were getting tougher and tougher by the day. Gina was advancing with all that good knowledge, although English grammar wouldn't stick up there; in her head.

On the weekends, reading, and if permitted, visiting the birds or the old house and frolicking in the fields, was the extent of her passing the long hours away.

As for Diane and her dummy pals; each day they behaved worse than the day previous. They were merciless towards Gina and their misdeeds became countless.

They had planted thumb-tacks for her to sit on. They would pour ketchup, mayonnaise, mustard, atop of her head; it didn't matter what the stuff was; the pepper being the worse. It had caused her to sneeze relentlessly, and she had suffered recurring nosebleeds. They would fake fights suitable to Miss Orr's arrival, and Gina always wound up as the instigator then was lashed. They had stolen several articles of her clothing; and she had found them on the floor, ripped to shreds. They tripped her in the hallways and on the staircases. They would pitch sorted, slimy foods at her; which Gina assumed Fanny had generously donated; especially the eggs and the peanut butter, they used to smear on her face.

Their latest fad is picking their schnozzles, then flipping the boogers at her. They just didn't give a damn...

Gina wanted to wring their necks. She hated them so! She thought them a bunch of gruesome, disgusting, ill-mannered ruffians. The poor people already in those insane asylums were safe, she thought. The really insane ones were out on the loose in this crazy house, and are driving her crazy.

Gina avoided telling Miss Alexis about many of the incidences, merely to keep harmony. She was scared those girls would turn against Miss Alexis and have her dismissed by Miss Adler.

The fall season was setting in. The leaves on the trees were shading to bright orange, red and yellow. Her befriended birds were slowly leaving their nests as the weather was becoming colder, and Gina brooded that she would never see them again.

The eve of Halloween, the girls dressed in colorful costumes. They masqueraded as ugly witches, skeletons and clowns. Others dressed as fierce animals, devils, hobos and nursery rhyme characters.

They were waiting for the buses to arrive and drive them into town for trick or treating. Gina pretended nothing troubled her, but within, she ached to take part.

A huge white polar bear neared her, growling. It was holding a large bag. Frightened, she backed away, until laughter sounded from behind the disguise. She realized it was Diane's stupid laugh. Diane raised her arm up, bag and all. Gina kept her sights on the bag when Diane tilted it and white flour emerged, covering Gina entirely to look like a ghost.

Miss Orr had entered the dormitory to inform the girls that the buses had arrived. She spied Gina standing in the mess of flour and lashed her for making the mess, then said. "You don't really think you're going with the girls? Do you? You're not deserving of such a privilege." Gina wept and went to bed.

Halloween Day, Miss Alexis surprised Gina with an orange, paper Mache pumpkin stuffed with sorted candies. Gina was so pleased, and munching on the candy, savored its flavor.

The winter was sneaking in. The trees had become barren. The green grass shriveled lifelessly and the birds had disappeared.

Came Thanksgiving Day, and glistening white snow had blanketed the ground. A special holiday dinner was being served in the cafeteria for the girls and their families.

Gina was ordered out of her chair and to follow Miss Orr to the kitchen. "You will sit on the floor." She said treating her like an animal.

Fanny kicked a little stool over to her and placed a tray of food before her that even an animal would pass up. "Enjoy, kid! Enjoy!" Fanny wasn't kidding. Gina stared at all that thick black grease, intended for gravy, and felt to puke right there.

Faintly, she was able to hear Miss Adler address herself and welcome the guests. They joined her in a little prayer then they dove into their grub.

The Christmas holidays were soon to descend. One evening, the girls were enthusiastically discussing creating crafts and ornaments. They intended to hang them on the Christmas trees that were being set up in special areas of the school by Mr. Holden.

They were also planning for the scheduled Christmas Eve, assembly program. Each dormitory would be participating. The presentations would pertain justly to Christmas.

Gina was sitting on the floor dreaming up a special Christmas card she could make up for Miss Alexis from her old coloring book. It was the thought that counted and she wanted to give her something just to let her know how much she loved and appreciated her. In the stillness of it all, Diane bellied, "Hey, Little Orphan Annie! Wouldn't you like to join us?"

She disregarded her and Diane flew into a tantrum. In a huff, she stomped over to her. She snatched Gina's coloring book and spitefully tore it in half.

"Why did you do that? I need my coloring book!"

Diane slapped her then threw the two halves into her face, galloping away. Gina couldn't understand her lunacy. Within a few minutes, Diane scuffled back and said, "I get so pissed off when you don't answer my questions... it makes me want to beat the shit out of you." She spit at her, then unscrewed the light bulb from Gina's lamp and purposely dropped it smashing to smithereens. Diane quickly dashed out the swinging doors while her dummy pals stood waiting in anticipation.

Diane returned with Miss Orr and accused Gina of tossing the light bulb at her because she hadn't answered a question quick enough.

"I didn't," Gina retorted and was smacked sharply in her face.

"She could have hurt me, Miss Orr." Diane said smirking, then trotted away gloating. Gina was lashed and left to clean the mess; shedding useless tears.

The following morning, on Gina's way to the spare room, she met up with Mr. Holden lugging a huge pine tree. He appeared so busy that she spoke a quick "Hello" and a "Merry Christmas" and he did likewise.

Miss Alexis was her usual cheerful self, and during class session thought they would draw and color paper decorations to hang on the miniature Christmas tree she had purchased; and together they did.

The entire faculty and the girls from all three dormitories were gathering into the auditorium for the Christmas Eve assembly scheduled program.

Dormitory One enacted the story "A Christmas Carol." Next to participate was dormitory two; Gina's dormitory.

The girls paraded in a crooked line across the stage, swinging their arms and sheepishly giggling. Miss Orr stepped up to the microphone and in a squeaky voice announced, "A little holiday insight linking the traditions and customs of other countries in the world shall be presented. Each girl is wearing the dress wear suitable to the country they are representing."

Several girls performed then Joyce stepped forward. She nervously kept pulling on those cauliflower ears of hers and began, "My," she shrilled a high note, as though her throat got stuck. "My country is Denmark; before any children go to bed, they climb the attic stairs and place a large bowl in front of the attic door. In the morning when the children investigate, they usually find a gift and the bowl is gone." She stepped backwards, then covering her eyes and giggling, she stepped forward and said, "Oh, yeah! I forgot! Porridge was in the bowl." Everyone howled in an uproar.

Other girls took their turns performing, then Diane stumbled over to the microphone. She kept swaying her arms, to and fro, then she blurted, "My country is Italy." She began fidgeting with her fingers and staring at the ceiling. "In Italy, they use the urn of faith instead of a tree. Each kid takes their turn to reach into the urn for a gift; some of those urns are empty. I'm still wondering why? I added that part." She chuckled so hard her fat blubber shook like jelly, and the audience engaged in hysterical laughter.

Christmas morning the girls were cheerfully singing Christmas carols in accordance to the chiming steeple bells. When they tired, they began blabbing about who would be receiving the finest gifts and the most. Their greediness mounted from year to year, Gina thought; irked.

Gina was making up her bed when suddenly, she heard a piercing scream, jolting her. Quickly, she glanced around and saw the little girl whom she had wanted to play with in the sandbox a long time ago, holding her hand to her eye as it oozed blood. She was shouting, "My eye! It's bleeding!"

Joyce being the closest to the girl rushed over to her "What happened to you, kid?" She asked excitedly.

"Somebody threw that wooden hanger," the little girl pointed towards the floor. "Oh, my eye hurts awful!"

Immediately, Janet rushed to get Miss Adler while the girls crowded around the injured girl.

Soon after, Miss Adler barged into the room. "Get out of my way," she panted, shoving herself past the girls. "What happened here?" She stood gaping at the little girl. "Why, you're seriously injured! Come, child, we must get you to a hospital." She guided the little girl, seemingly unconcerned for an explanation. Suddenly, she stopped short and said, "Don't think this matter is over! I shall return." Her voice was stern.

During breakfast, everyone appeared edgy and chatted excessively about the incident. "Attention, please," a loud voice sounded. Quickly everyone silenced and glanced towards the bitch box (as the girls called it). It protruded outwardly from the center wall near the kitchen. "Due to the unfortunate accident,Miss Adler has advised that no one will be going home for the Christmas holidays," the voice informed. "You'll advise your parents as such when they visit at noontime today. Thank you!" the voice faded, then instantly the girls left for the dormitory wearing pouting faces.

The big circular clock which hung above the doorway showed the time was 12:50 p.m. when Miss Adler stormed into the dormitory. She appeared hot under the collar. Gina was frightened half to death watching her pace the floor from one end of the room to the other in utter silence. Her back and shoulders were hunched. Her arms were folded across her middle and her face was red as a beet. Her bushy eyebrows slightly quivered, and her mouth edged distortedly as she muttered under her breath. She looked up from the floor and came to a dead stand, hollering, "Who did it? Who did it? I want to know!" she scared the living daylights out of Gina. "Who threw the hanger? One of you insolent girls did it. I permit you to get away with a lot, but not this!" She choked on her saliva. "If I don't find out I'llpunish everyone severely," she moved to each girl, searching their faces, including Gina's. She wanted to hide under the bed and disappear "The child had to have seven stitches to close the wound! She nearly lost her eye; her parents are angry. If I have to stand here all day, I'll find out who did it."

The girls eyed each other with uncertainty. Tension was mounting, when suddenly, Gina heard Diane's voice excitedly, "She did it, Miss Adler!" She pointed to Gina.

"Yeah! Miss Adler she did it. I saw her throw the hanger." Joyce fibbed.

"Me and Janet saw her do it too, Miss Adler," Tina stuck her two cents in. Gina grew fearful as Diane babbled, "I didn't want to snitch, but, I don't want to be punished for something I didn't do."Tears filled Gina's eyes as she expected to hear all the girls accuse her as well, but oddly they remained silent.

Like a tigress, Miss Adler scurried over to Gina. She backed herself on to her bed in panic trying to elude her reach. "I didn't do it! I didn't throw nothing!" She cried out.

Forcefully, Miss Adler grasped her wrist, dragging her off the bed then threw a sharp punch to her face, knocking her to the floor. "Despicable child! Wretched liar!" she unfastened her ruler, lashing crazily at her body. "When I get through with you, Miss Prissy, you'll never, never lie again. She grunted with every swat.

"Don't! No more! Don't hit me no more!" Blood seeped from everywhere.

"You are worse than the devil himself! Get off that floor!" Gina struggled to stay afoot as her head whirled and her body felt on fire. "You have committed a grave act and you shall be put in confinement." Now, out into that hallway with you; liven it up too." She wacked her legs. "I haven't got all day! Move faster!" Gina limped her way and heard Miss Adler say, "Girls, I'm sorry your morning has been upsetting, but Miss Prissy will be taken care of! You have my word! Thank you, Diane, for speaking up. Have a Merry Christmas."

"Miss Adler, does this mean we can go home? I'm bored," Diane asked.

"No one may go home until this matter is settled," Miss Adler trotted out into the hallway. "Follow me, Miss Prissy," she fastened her ruler.

Gina wobbled down a staircase, around it, then under the stairwell. Miss Adler unlocked a door then nudged her into a small room. It smelled of mildew and felt cold and damp. Darkness was evident, except for the sunlight peeping through a wee window. A cot, a nightstand which sat a lamp atop of it, set adjacent to a washstand and a commode. The walls showed deep cracks and the paint peeling. "This is where you'll spend your Christmas Day." Miss Adler remarked.

"Miss Adler," Gina dared speak, sniffling. "Diane lied. I didn't throw no hanger! Why don't you ever believe me?" Her tears flowed.

"Do you dare to criticize my judgment?" She angrily slapped her. "If I feel humble, I'll have Fanny bring you some toast. I shall deal with you in the morning." She darted off.

Gina was trembling greatly. Her hands were shaky. She couldn't control her tears. She was locked in this hole like an animal and felt she'd gone crazy. She couldn't take the abuse any longer, and had fallen apart; it was like the end of the road for her. Unthinking, she merely brushed away the cockroaches off the washstand and crazily kept scooping up water in her hand, throwing it at herself; supposedly rinsing off the blood from her wounds.

She sat on the cot dazed. She was frightened as hell! She slipped off her shoes and placed them under the pillow. She felt chilled. She reached for the blanket that smelled of rot and dampness, wrapping herself, then laid down. Miss Alexis's words came to haunt her. "Be strong! Keep hoping! Forgive!"And she cried more bitterly, falling asleep.

CHAPTER TEN

Daylight was still peeping through the wee window when Gina was awakened by the sound of the door latch clicking. She watched the door push open and saw Miss Orr standing in the threshold, looking googol eyed. "Come with me," she spoke hostile. "Miss Adler expects you in her office this morning."

Gina was confused. She hadn't realized she'd slept until morning; and seeing daylight peering through the wee window, she thought it was late afternoon.

She hopped off the cot and began to fold the blanket. "Never mind that. Get your shoes on."

"Is it really morning, Miss Orr?"

"Of course! What's wrong with you anyway? Hurry it up! We haven't got all day."

She hurriedly reached for her shoes from under the pillow. She followed Miss Orr outdoors. She was a sad sight; all blood stained and her dress damp and wrinkled. Her jaw ached, and upon touching it she felt swelling.

She was without a jacket and felt frozen by the time they arrived inside the main building, and into the office. "Miss Adler, here she is." Miss Orr called.

"Thank you," Miss Adler expressed then directed her attention to Gina. "You'll sit on a chair over there, in the waiting area until I call for you," she quickly disappeared into a side office, slamming the door behind her.

Gina was a bundle of nerves. Her head was aching and her stomach hurt; it began rumbling. She was scared. Frightful thoughts hovered her mind. Her tears flowed easily when she heard, "Gina, come in here," Miss Adler called.

She was stymied hearing her name called. Miss Adler had never called her Gina before. She walked over to her. Upon entering an office, she viewed three women wearing the same apparel as Miss Adler. They were sitting beside one another graciously smiling at her. Scared out of her wits, and anticipating a severe scolding and whipping or even confinement in that hell hole, she concealed her tear filled eyes with her hands.

"Counselors, this is Gina Haskol," Miss Adler introduced.

"Gina, don't hide your eyes. We're not going to hurt you." A counselor assured. She took her hand away from her eyes, guiding Gina over to her.

"Counselors, I'm sorry I had to call upon you at this time. You know with the holidays and all." Miss Adler commented. "As you know, I had been advised to call upon you to appease the Kelloggs; they expect justification regarding their child's injury, and now that we have the culprit here we can proceed with the questions.

Gina's tears flowed!

"Now, now, dear! There is no reason for tears. We are here to learn the truth concerning yesterday's accident," the same counselor said, patting Gina's hands. Through her tears she noticed an odd look come over the counselors face as she examined her entirely, bruises and all. However, she made no waves concerning anything.

"Gina, I am Miss Tyler. Beside me is Miss Borden and beside her, is Miss Holly." Miss Tyler introduced.

Gina sniffled a sheepish, "Hello," as she casually slipped her hands from Miss Tyler's clasp.

"Gina, how old are you?" Miss Tyler asked.

"I'm-I'm 11, but, I'll be 12 soon," Gina stuttered.

Miss Tyler asked her to relate all she could regarding the accident and that she expected truthfulness.

She was uptight and fearful relating the events. She cried in between sentences and excluded Miss Adler, the girls and the confinement. "I didn't do it! I didn't do it!" She cried. "I wouldn't hurt nobody! I didn't throw no hanger!"

"If you didn't, why were you accused?"

She hesitated to reply. She exchanged glances with Miss Adler and sensed her icy stare to convey. Keep your mouth shut, she thought to herself. She was trembling and frightened to say anything more.

Miss Tyler recognized her fear, pledging no harm would come to her.

Gina trusted her words and exposed Diane and her dummy pals, unfolding the horrible torment and abuse they had put her through.

"Don't ask me no more! I'm afraid! No more!" She panicked and wept uncontrollably.

"Dear! Dear! It's alright. What are you afraid of? Tell us! We want to help you if we can." and in the same breath Miss Tyler said, "Miss Adler, what has this child to fear?"

"I suppose Diane." Miss Adler calmly replied.

"That may be true, but I fear there is much more behind this child's tears, and I intend to find out." She handed Gina her handkerchief to wipe her sniffles, then, wanting for Gina to reveal more about Diane and her pals.

Gina's mind was in a frenzy; one minute she felt she could trust the counselors, and the next minute she feared they were only being kind to trick her. She was downright scared! She lowered her head, and feeling her warm tears fall upon her bruised hands, reminding her of her misery, unwavering, she described Diane's twisted lies; and her pals Joyce, Janet and Tina; even lie for her.

"Tell me Gina! Was there any particular girl at any time who was nice to you?" Miss Holly asked, changing the subject.

Her question threw Gina as Ellen's note flashed before her. She looked up at Miss Holly and biting her quivering lip, she gave an account of Ellen; a girl she doesn't know; or ever knew; She doesn't even know what she looks like, but she had sneaked a friendly note to her once; Because the note was precious to Gina, she saved it. "I'll show you," she took off her shoe, pulled out the note, and handed it to Miss Tyler.

She took time out to read the note then passed it on to Miss Borden. When all three counselors were through reading they glanced at one another, wearing a look of amazement upon their faces.

Miss Adler moved about restlessly in her chair. "Is all this fool questioning necessary?" She sputtered. "We know the child caused the accident so why not come to a conclusion and end this useless interrogation?"

"No, Miss Adler! We're not so sure the child really caused the injury!" Miss Tyler remarked. "As I previously stated, I feel there is a great deal more behind this child's tears; we have learned quite a bit already." Her words were encouraging, but Gina remained fearful.

"Gina. Do you like your classes? Are you learning?" Miss Borden quizzed.

Although tears were streaming down her face, Gina seemed to glow as she elaborated about Miss Alexis being her special tutor and how much she loves her; how kind she is; and all her wonderful teachings. Especially, how Miss Alexis told her to always tell the truth.

Miss Tyler interrupted voicing, "Miss Adler, why does Gina have a special tutor? It doesn't exist in this school. She should have been placed in regular classes with the other girls. Something is very wrong here!" She jotted in her folder. "According to our office records, Gina doesn't exist."

"Perhaps her files were lost!" Miss Adler quickly intervened.

"We were unaware of the matter until this incident arose. We searched through stacks of files and listings of tuition fees, but found nothing. Yes, something is very wrong, isn't that so, Miss Adler?"

The blood seemed to drain from Miss Adler's face, and from what little Gina could understand, it sounded as though Miss Adler was in a heap of trouble. "We'll get to that later, but can we put an end to this wishy-washy, question and answer game?" Miss Adler spoke brazenly. "I can't see the importance of it all."

"We'll not put an end to it, Miss Adler," Miss Tyler retorted. "Your impatience is uncalled for; the child deserves the right to clear herself, and we intend to give it to her." Her aggressiveness frightened Gina. She grew tense and her tears would not cease. "Gina, I'm going to ask you a very important question, and I expect a truthful reply." Gina found herself gazing into Miss Tyler's spritely blue eyes in wonder. "When Diane and her friends would accuse you of an incident, were you punished? If so, what method of punishment was used and who did the punishing?"

Gina froze hearing the question. She felt like all four walls were closing in on her. She was scared to death to tell the honest truth. She feared being beaten and confined in that hell hole; even starved. Her thoughts stirred frantically when suddenly, she began shaking uncontrollably and crazily screaming, "I can't tell you that! I can't! I can't! Please don't ask me no more."

"Gina, Gina," Miss Tyler reached out for her, drawing her close. "What is it? Such a little girl should not fear as you do! Are you afraid of getting punished if you tell the truth? Well, let me assure you, dear that won't happen. Believe me!"

Gina stood weeping and gulping. She was consumed with fear. In the midst of it all, she suddenly thought of Miss Alexis's words, seemingly giving her strength. When she felt Miss Tyler's fingers massaging the bruises on the back of her hand, and remembering how they got there, unfaltering, she began to disclose the answers to Miss Tyler's questions.

"The child lies! The child lies!" Miss Adler fumed. "You don't actually believe her lies? She is a habitual liar. I feel you all best know this."

Miss Adler's outburst fused Gina's innards. She was scared all right, but knew she was telling the truth. She had to fight back. She'd gone this far and all that mattered was the truth. She didn't care anymore when she blurted out, "I'm not lying! I don't lie! You both did beat me; so did the girls; you almost let me die too!" Hysterically crying, she jerked herself out of Miss Tyler's grasp. Her mind was reacting crazily and daringly. Unexpectedly, she extended both her arms outwardly for all three counselors to view. "Look! Look at all the cuts! That's from the ruler." She stepped back a ways. "And look! Look at my legs all cut up." She lifted her dress allowing them to see further. "She did most of it yesterday. She even punched my face and put me in a little room filled with cockroaches!" She cried her little heart out and unaccountably flung herself to the floor beside Miss Tyler, wearily rocking herself.

The room fell hushed except for Gina's faint sighs and gurgles. The counselors began whispering amongst themselves and in a while, Miss Tyler spoke, "Miss Adler, we don't believe that Gina threw the hanger that caused the injury; it appears there is more to this matter than meets the eye."

The counselors seemed to be getting down to the nitty-gritty when in a rage, Miss Adler accused Gina of having fabricated everything; claiming her bruises had stemmed from a fight; and yes, she did confine her as punishment. She insisted that Gina was wise and foxy and could con anyone with her insincere tears.

"No, Miss Adler, the child does not lie!" Miss Tyler said. "Perhaps I should explain. Gina was questioned to evaluate an unbelievable tale which was told to us in confidence; please be assured that we counselors were definitely uncertain of its validity, due to the source from which we obtained the information." She cleared her throat. "However, Gina's answers coincided accurately with the information we had obtained, that there is no doubt in our minds that the story revealed to us is indeed,the truth; just looking at her appearance is shameful."

Miss Adler glared heatedly at the counselors for a spell, then exploded, "How can you allegedly sit there and tell me you believe a child's lies and false information! You dare oppose my word! This school has a fine reputation, and I have been here many years accomplishing its good standing." She slammed her hand on the desk.

"This is true and the school is highly recommended," Miss Tyler conceded. "However, what lies before us has nothing to do with school merits or reputation; the facts are we have a serious case of child abuse and neglect."

"Child abuse! Neglect! What are you implying?"

"Exactly what I stated... Child abuse! Not only has the child been abused by adults, but by the girls as well, which makes you,

Miss Adler twice as guilty for not putting an end to the girls hostility immediately. Miss Adler, why did you permit it?"

Miss Adler found herself in a bind. It was her turn to retaliate. "Oh, you know kids," she giggled slightly. "They can be catty and selfish, but it was all harmless bickering in fun and play. Wasn't it Gina?"

Gina seemed to be in a rambling frame of mind; just sitting and rocking. She acknowledged the question by simply shaking her head "No!"

"May I ask you where the information you have gathered derived from?" Miss Adler asked.

"That you may," on that note, Gina's ears perked a bit and saw Miss Tyler checking her wristwatch. "You'll have your answer shortly, Miss Adler! I am expecting guests and they should be in the front office; Excuse me for a moment."

Gina could hear a mouse squeak it was so quiet, when she heard voices nearing. She glanced toward the doorway and was surprised to see the little girl who was injured. She was wearing a small white patch above her eye. She entered the room and took position, standing beside Gina. An attractive couple followed. "Gina, Miss Adler, meet Mr. and Mrs. Kellogg." Miss Tyler introduced. "Miss Adler, I believe you spoke with Mrs. Kellogg over the phone!"

"That's correct." Miss Adler commented then rose from her chair and hastily brought forward two chairs. "Please sit." She invited the Kellogg's.

"Gina!' Miss Tyler called. "The young girl standing beside you is Ellen." she introduced.

At that moment, Gina shuddered. A cold chill raced through her, wondering if Ellen was the same girl who had written her the note. Could it really be her, she thought.

Miss Tyler resumed the inquest, reminding Miss Adler of her earlier question then informed, "Your answer sits before you."

"I presumed as such," Miss Adler snapped.

"I will explain briefly how the information was acquired, then we can go on from there. The counselors and I found it necessary to secure information from Ellen regarding her injury. Therefore, we visited the Kellogg's home yesterday afternoon. While I was conversing with Ellen, she had asked me quite innocently, who was blamed for throwing the hanger. I opened my folder and replied, Gina Haskol. I'd noticed that the mention of Gina's name brought tears to Ellen's eyes, which troubled me. I heard Ellen mumble, "Poor Gina! Miss Adler must have beaten her to a pulp." I asked her what she meant by her remark, but she clammed up. Her parent's urged her to speak up, and when she was through relating her story, we were astonished to learn about the abuse which Gina had been subjected to."

At that point, Miss Tyler reminded Miss Adler of the statement made earlier that the counselors, and herself had not validated the tale, and for this reason they saw fit to seek out the truth.

Mrs. Kellogg saw fit to voice her thoughts to Miss Adler characterizing that whenever Ellen was at home, for holidays and such, she worried terribly about Gina and all the abuse and harassing she would sustain; and just because the child is an orphan. "Terribly cruel, Miss Adler." she remarked. "Ellen wanted to make friends with Gina, but because of a youngster named Diane, Ellen was not permitted to associate. I disliked hearing about it. Many times I felt I should report the problem, but then I would tell myself, who would ever believe Ellen? A child's word!"

"I take it you believed Ellen?" Miss Adler asked.

"We certainly did. Ellen wouldn't, out of the blue, make up such a horrible tale."

Miss Adler's response to Mrs. Kellogg was that Gina was always a troublesome child, and disciplinary measures had to be taken. She admitted tapping Gina with the ruler at times, but not enough to hurt her.

"That's not true, Miss Adler, and you know it!" Ellen lashed out, startling everyone. "I watched you and Miss Orr whack and hit Gina every day; thanks to Diane and her dumb friends. I watched her cry and bleed. It made me sad. No one cared what happened to her. I even wrote her a note once just to comfort her and let her know she had a friend. I never told her who I was; just because of that pain, Diane. I sure wish Miss Alexis were here; she could tell plenty; Miss Tyler knows." Her bright blue eyes swelled with tears, staring at the floor.

"You exaggerate, young lady! In this school we maintain discipline to the utmost, and I asserted every measure upon Gina which I felt necessary."

"Necessary!" Ellen cried out. "You call giving her shiners necessary? What about when they cut her pretty long hair? And you wouldn't believe she was sick; almost letting her die! She never deserved what you, the girls, and Miss Orr dished out to her. Fanny too! You're all mean and cruel."

"Ellen, that was disrespectful. Apologize." Mrs. Kellogg reprimanded.

"I'm sorry, but it's true!" Ellen spoke no further.

The counselors chatted awhile when Miss Tyler voiced, "Ellen! Thank you for that strong and sensitive version. It has aided us stupendously in reaching a final conclusion. Both yours and Gina's facts coincided harmoniously." She expressed, reverting her attention to Miss Adler. "Now, Miss Adler, in our judgment, we find Gina not guilty." Miss Tyler stroked Gina's head. "We are sure someone else did the dirty work and used Gina as the scapegoat; and I'm determined to find out."

Miss Adler was on her last leg and in a fury accused the youngsters of collaborating their stories. "Their lies have placed her in a most embarrassing position." She exclaimed. "I don't take lightly to the accusation of which I have been accused. I say Gina is guilty!"

"The girls don't lie, Miss Adler." Miss Tyler huffed. "You can't beat around the bush anymore. You, Miss Orr, and those four youngsters are the culprits! Not Gina! We were unsure of Gina's truthfulness, all the way, but when she mentioned the friend she never knew and gave us Ellen's note to read...well, the note played an important role; it beheld the truth, and I'm certainly glad that Gina kept it."

"The note is hog-wash! I'm not guilty of anything! Ellen spoke falsely! She's just stirring up trouble; a situation which has never existed."

"Miss Adler, examine your conscience because the truth lies there." Miss Holly hadn't minced words. "You have caused Gina much needless suffering and pain. You stand accused of child abuse and neglect; and perhaps other demeanors. All you have worked for will go totally down the drain. You shall repent!" Miss Adler had met her waterloo!

Gina quietly listened to everyone chit-chat about, "If Ellen hadn't been injured, Gina's situation would have never come to light; How amazing that Gina had kept her sanity; the real culprit would be found out; and isn't it strange how the Almighty works in mysterious ways." They went on and on.

Judging from the conversation, Gina had become aware that the hell she'd lived in was burning its final ash and that her little body and her mind would finally find peace. Miss Alexis's words of wisdom had become a reality!

Tearfully, Gina caught Ellen's attention. They exchanged warm smiles and words were needless when Gina easily took hold of Ellen's hand, squeezing it gently. It was her way to convey her heartwarming gratitude to a friend who cared enough to help her in the time of need.

The Kellogg's had departed and Miss Adler sat, resting her head in her hands, swaying slightly. It was the end of the road for her, and three years too late to say I'm sorry...her day of reckoning had arrived. Strangely, as Gina watched her helplessly swaying, she felt compassion for her, but she wasn't sure why?

CHAPTER ELEVEN

"Excuse me, Miss Tyler. Miss Borden said. "I suggest that Miss Adler speak with everyone regarding this matter. I trust It'll eliminate future problems; those girls will naturally be hostile as usual; perhaps an assembly can be scheduled?"

"You're correct, Miss Borden, but not just yet." Miss Tyler replied. "I have a thought in mind. I don't Intend leaving any strings unattached."

The lunch bell sounded and Miss Tyler suggested that both girls go to lunch together.

"But what about the girls?" Ellen reminded.

"No need to worry about them, dear. We'll be right behind you watching and listening."

"Miss Borden! The thought I had in mind will take effect as of now." Miss Tyler said. "We three are going to do a little undercover work," she grinned slyly. "Assembly will come later. I do believe you both get my drift."

"Oh, we do!" The counselors giggled.

"C'mon, little one! It's time to be happy!" Miss Tyler called to Gina, stretching her arms outwardly. "Grab hold of my hands," she yanked and Gina flew into her arms, slightly smiling.

"Oh, Miss Tyler, thank you!" Gina hugged her tightly. "Thank you for believing--and Miss Borden. You too, Miss Holly. Thank you for giving me my friend Ellen!"

"Crying is all over, dear, thanks to Ellen," Miss Holly said. "There are happier days ahead."

"Now go to lunch, girls, and remember, act normal; just be yourselves. We'll be on your tail," Miss Tyler reminded them and they walked happily on their way. As they furthered out the office, they heard Miss Tyler say, "Well, counselors, if things are the way the girls say they are, we should get some results. I just have a feeling we might. So, let's go!" the girls heard the door slam shut, leaving Miss Adler to her woes.

As the girls stepped outdoors the cold air felt exuberating to Gina. She felt free and jubilant, "Oh, Ellen, I'm so happy," she shouted then bent down and printed in the snow:

"THANK YOU, MY DEAR FRIEND ELLEN."

They commenced to merrily walk hand-in-hand and when they arrived at the doorway of the cafeteria, Gina glanced over her shoulder, noticing the three counselors slowly pacing their way. The girls were already seated and chowing down their food when Gina and Ellen walked over to the kitchen counter.

While Fanny was serving Ellen a delicious looking platter of roast beef, mashed potatoes, with all the goodies, Gina spotted Miss Tyler hiding behind the back kitchen door. Ellen walked off a ways, waiting for Gina when Fanny spouted, "Well, who let you out of your cage, kid? I see Miss Adler roughed you up but good! You deserved worse." She began slopping her food.

"You there, serving! Come here, instantly," Miss Tyler called angrily.

Fanny startled and her eyes widened big as marbles. The platter shook in her hand as she set it on the counter, then she took giant steps over to Miss Tyler; Gina couldn't hear the conversation, but noticed Fanny's rosy cheeks had turned pale and her head kept bobbing up and down like a yo-yo. When Miss Tyler was through chewing her out, she hurriedly returned and was shaking like a leaf as she picked up a clean platter, spooning Gina's food (fit for a queen). Sighting her food looking so tasty, she felt so happy that her throat lumped, but did manage to thank Fanny.

As they began to ramble towards Gina's assigned table, she was feeling kind of tense. She slyly turned and saw Miss Tyler watching to see where they would be sitting. They sat with their backs to Diane and her dummy pals.

Soon after, loud-mouth Diane stood up and shouted, "Hey, you dummies! Little Orphan Annie is back and, look! She found herself a hound dog." She patted Ellen's head. "Hey, skunk! Did Miss Adler beat and slug you in the cage like she did in the dormitory? We sure framed you but good!"

Inconspicuously, Gina looked for Miss Tyler and sighted her peeping through the slightly opened door that was situated close by her table but was seldom used. She nudged Ellen's arm and whispered, "Over there by that door." Ellen nodded her head understandingly.

"You know skunk, I have myself and my dummy pals to thank for yesterday's foul up; if you really want to know, I flung the hanger at you skunk, but the damn thing went cockeyed; sorry about that, hound dog." Diane bopped Ellen on the head, and Gina eyed her a bit concerned. "No matter though--you got blamed and that's all I care about." Gina and Ellen eyed each other realizing Miss Tyler's ears must be perking.

Momentarily, Diane neared Ellen, grabbing the nape of her neck. Ellen cringed as Diane said, "You, hound dog, don't belong here with the skunk! No one sits with that thing! So get your ass the hell out!"

Ellen stayed put and Diane began to pull on her, then her pals joined in practically carting Ellen out of her chair, when Gina saw the side door being flung open and Miss Tyler came charging in a dead heat towards the table. "All of you! Take your hands off of that child immediately," she shrilled, scaring the hell out of everyone, and almost causing the girls to dump Ellen to the floor.

The room fell silent and Gina was able to hear the steam pipes hissing away. There was no joking! No laughter! No abuse! The girls wore astonished expressions across their faces and all eyes were directed at Miss Tyler as she voiced, "You there! The brazen one who calls herself Diane! Come out here and snap to it," Diane bounced her way in a frenzy. "So you say the hanger you threw at Ellen yesterday, which was supposedly meant for Gina, went cockeyed huh! Well, we'll just see how much bullying you do later."

Instantly, Miss Orr rushed over, "Diane is correct. The youngster with the long hair doesn't belong at that table; she sits elsewhere," Miss Orr explained. "Diane helps me monitor and she was doing her job. I heard Diane tell the child to remove herself, but the child refused to budge; Diane was doing her best."

"You really think so?" Miss Tyler infuriated, placing her hands to her hips. "And which nursemaid are you?"

I'm Miss Orr. I'm in charge of dormitory two."

"And I am Miss Tyler, Counselor and Director of the Board of Advisory. My associates behind me are Miss Borden and Miss Holly," sighs of bewilderment buzzed throughout the cafeteria.

"Before you speak further, Miss Orr, I suggest you engage your brain in gear. You're fretting to shield Diane is over! So don't try to buffalo me!"

Miss Orr stood agape, shocked. Those eyeballs of hers seemed jet propelled as she excitedly responded, "I was only insisting what I believe to be true. Diane was doing her job as usual!"

"You think so? Why the profanity I heard pouring out from that trash mouth of hers was atrocious, and you have the nerve to tell me she was doing her job! Let me inform you--it has ceased as of now." Miss Tyler looked at Diane. "Do I make myself clear, young lady?" Diane nodded her head, smirking cowardly "Now, Diane, I want you to call out your three friends; I do believe you know what I'm referring to!"

Diane stood staring at the floor, dragging one leg then the other and said, "I don't want to. I'm no stool pigeon."

"How dare you defy a request! Your behavior is disrespectful and loathsome." Miss Tyler wacked her suddenly in the face so hard that Diane's head rocked. She was stunned and her eyes watered; something Gina had never witnessed. The tables had turned! "Now call your friends, or shall I. You are not protecting anyone by trying to be a martyr."

Diane appeared deep in thought. She'd been humiliated in front of her idols. She was put down and cut to size, and her bed of roses had lost their fragrance. In a solemn tone of voice, she spurted, "Joyce, Janet, Tina, c'mon." They rose from their seats, looking pale and glassy eyed, marching over to MissTyler. Gina could feel the fear within them. She'd been there a thousand times. "And Gina shall be called Gina! Understand?" Miss Tyler emphasized.

"You four have been a disgrace to this school, including yourself, Miss Orr. You've unmercifully crucified that child and I can't bear the thought of the pain she's suffered." Miss Tyler pointed to Gina.

"You've almost succeeded in driving her to the brink of madness, and your inhumane actions shall be accounted for; so get your tails moving and follow me. You too, Miss Orr." The group trampled away with their heads lowered, and when they were out of sight, the girls began to whisper curiously among themselves, but kept their distance.

Gina realized that the truth had paved a happier path for her to flourish and, although she was just a mere youngster, she also realized she would live a lifetime of horrid memories.

In a while, a voice sounded over the bitch-box, and the room quieted. "Today at three o'clock this afternoon assembly is scheduled. The entire school, staff and faculty shall be present. Thank you!" Quickly everyone set to gabbing again, when Miss Holly approached Gina and Ellen.

"Gina! Ellen! Miss Tyler advised that you'll not have to attend assembly. Have a fine day, girls." She left cheerfully.

"Thank you, Miss Holly," they harmonized to her, then joyfully took off for the spare room.

"It's so good to hear you laugh, Gina." Ellen said. "I'm so glad my parents made me talk with the counselors. I should have said something a long time ago, but like my mom said... who would believe a kid!"

Time seemed to have flown. The clock above the doorway in the library showed 3:50 p.m. "I wonder what's happening in assembly?" Gina mentioned.

"I was wondering, too! I guess we'll find out later." Ellen replied.

"I bet'cha Diane and those dummy pals of hers try to worm themselves out of everything."

"I suppose, but I don't think Miss Tyler will fall for their bull. She won't let them off that easy, Ellen remarked and the remainder of the afternoon they browsed through picture books; and for the first time Gina was a normal kid again; just enjoying kid's fun.

The supper bell sounded, and both girls pranced to the cafeteria carefree from ugly thoughts, but Gina felt that tension gripping her again as they stood in line waiting to be served. The girls acted flustered, as though they didn't know how to handle themselves towards Gina. Some passed by her saying, "Hi!" Others approached her in groups stating, "We're really sorry!"

Fanny looked like she had gone through the mill. Her eyes showed red circles around them and her skin appeared blotchy. No doubt she'd been crying. Gina thought and noticed she was yet shaky when dishing out her food; and in the fashion it should have been doled, a long time ago.

Both girls meandered to Gina's table. Gina glanced over her shoulder, and saw Diane walking over to her table. Her eyes were reddened, and the cocky smirk she always wore showed no longer. Strangely, all the girls welcomed her with icy stares and cold shoulders.

"She probably expected her usual three cheers for Diane, welcome," Ellen stated.

A short while passed when Joyce piped up, "You know Diane, we wouldn't be in this mess if you had left the orphan alone from the start. Now our parents are going to find out, and boy, oh boy, what a pickle I'll be in. I don't look forward to that! You thought you were so smart! You had to be top dog! The big fat show-off! The big cheese!" She was steaming. "You thought you were hot shit on a stick, but it turned out you're only a cold fart on a toothpick."

"You weren't so innocent either, Joyce. You were just as rotten as Diane!" Janet implied.

"Yeah, I admit it, but I'll tell you something! If Diane hadn't started picking on the orphan, I don't think that I would have done the things I did; I took advantage of a readymade situation and went along with it because I was scared of Diane. Yeah, I admit it. I didn't want to be her enemy. I saw what she did to the orphan from the start; boy, am I ever sorry I did what I did!"

"Hey, Joyce, her name is Gina! Remember what Miss Tyler said about calling her by her real name?" Several girls shouted.

"That's why I followed!" Janet remarked. "I felt the same as you did Joyce; scared--just plain scared."

"Me, too," Tina admitted. "Miss Tyler said, she wasn't expelling us because our tuition fees are paid, but we won't be receiving graduation diplomas. My mom is going to kill me!"

"Boy, Miss Tyler sure hollered at Miss Adler and Miss Orr," Janet said. "I never thought I'd see tears in their eyes. They're going to be expelled! Can you imagine?"

"Yeah! Diane cried her eyeballs out," Joyce said. "Miss Tyler even mentioned a possible law suit because of Ellen's eye; and because we lied about it we might be dragged into it! Boy, we sure stepped into a glob of shit and I'm scared."

"I wish I hadn't ever laughed at Gina now." A girl hollered, and all the girls shouted their similar regrets.

Diane appeared drowned in thought when in a huff she slid herself away from the table. She picked up her tray and trotted over to an unoccupied table and sat sulking.

"She's getting a dose of her own medicine," Ellen sparked. "My mother always says that! Think about it, Gina; she's hurt you all these years; well, it's about time she knew what it feels like to be put down and cast aside like an animal. I don't feel sorry for her either."

CHAPTER TWELVE

Gina never really learned the valued words of wisdom that had transpired during assembly or in Miss Adler's office, but since that miraculous day, conditions were altered.

The days sped by, bringing in the New Year. Joy was written all over Miss Alexis's face when she entered the spare room, embracing Gina. "Miss Tyler spoke with me, and I revealed all." She mentioned. "I was so thrilled to learn of the justifiable events. You certainly have a friend in Ellen."

"Oh, Miss Alexis, you don't know all the bad things that happened, but I thought of you and it gave me lots of strength." Gina related. "Miss Alexis, when the three counselors were questioning me, Miss Tyler told Miss Adler that I wasn't supposed to have a tutor. She said something about me not being on file and that I didn't exist. Did Miss Tyler say anything to you about it?"

"Yes she did mention it to me, dear. It appears that Miss Adler never registered you through proper channels--within the main office. Naturally your name wouldn't appear in the files."

"Why didn't she register me?"

"It's a confusing situation, dear. Miss Adler refuses to commit herself. It appears that the monies and tuition fees received, supposedly for your care; it was going into someone else's pocket other than the school. Presently, Miss Tyler can only assume that Miss Adler is the culprit."

"You mean she may have cheated and stolen?"

"It's a possibility, dear. If Miss Adler is truly the culprit, she just never thought her scheme would backfire. I sure wish I was certain about the entire matter. It would explain her reasons for not wanting me to meddle in her affairs regarding yourself."

"Maybe it's the reason why she never bought me any clothing or anything!"

"That is an understatement, dear! Well, whatever, Miss Tyler is investigating further."

Several days remained before the closing of the third semester. Gina was lying on her bed, and let her thoughts drift to the day she would be leaving the school. Where would she be placed next? Would she be placed in another school? Would she be placed in a foster home? And if so, would they like her or be mean to her?

"Gina," she heard Miss Alexis call. "Can you come to the library with me for a while?"

"Yes, Miss Alexis." She hopped off her bed. "You look so sad! Why?"

"I'm not really, dear." Gina noticed her eyes moisten. When they arrived in the spare room, Miss Alexis sat Gina on her lap. "I'm going to miss you, Gina," she blurted.

"Why do you say that, Miss Alexis? I'll be leaving this school too, and I'll miss you a whole bunch, but we're not leaving each other yet!"

"I am though. I'm going far away, dear, out of the country."

"Why so far away? Won't I ever see you again?"

"I'm going to unite with the missionaries and help the needy people. I'll be taking an early flight tomorrow morning.

"Early tomorrow morning! Oh, Miss Alexis, I'll be lost without you! I'll need you forever; even when I grow up."

"I waited till this evening to tell you so it wouldn't be so difficult for either of us; I'll write you, I promise. I told Miss Tyler to forward your new address to me wherever you might settle."

"Will you really write me?"

"I promise. I'll always want to know how my little girl is doing."

She opened the top drawer of her desk, retrieving a circular box.

"That's a pretty red box. It looks like my blue one I keep my trinkets in."

"This is the gift I'd promised to bring back for you before I'd left for the Christmas holidays," Miss Alexis reminded Gina, handing it to her. "I held on to it so that I could give it to you at this special time."

Upon opening the box, she viewed a tiny piece of gold jewelry. "It's my name written in gold and it has two shiny stones!" Gina spoke excitedly.

"I had it inscribed especially for you. The little stones are diamond chips which represents your birthstone for April. It's a pin you can always wear."

"Oh, Miss Alexis it's so pretty. I'll take good care of it; just like the cross and chain; see I'm still wearing it." She hugged her tightly. "Oh, I wish you weren't going so far away. I'm scared, Miss Alexis. I'm leaving here in a few days, and I don't know what's going to happen to me." She began to weep.

"Gina, dear, please don't cry. Just remember, dear, when you go out into the world try to be happy. Always be kind to others! I realize you'll never forget the misery and rejection you experienced here but try to put it behind you; learn to love life; grasp and treasure it. Never renounce what you dearly prize; and infinitely hope for whatever is righteous; never despair."

"I love you, Miss Alexis, but I feel I'm losing you; it's just like before I came to this school; I told you about my lady friend

Annie—I loved her too, but she never came back; I lost her, and I don't want to lose you too."

"It's the way of life, dear, and what the Almighty destines we must accept. Now it's getting late and I must prepare for my flight in the morning." She slid Gina off her lap. "You be a real good girl. I'll always love you, dear and I'll write," she embraced and kissed her lovingly. "Goodbye, Gina dear." She turned to leave.

"I'm afraid! I'm afraid, Miss Alexis! Do you have to go?" Gina darted after her, nestling up to her. "I'll always remember and love you. I wish you didn't have to go!" she cried one last time in her embrace. "Goodbye, Miss Alexis. I love you." Gina felt like dying as she exited the library forever.

In the morning, while Gina was making up her bed, Ellen neared her and said, "Gina, why so glum?

What's the matter? You're usually so happy."

"Miss Alexis went away today. She took a plane early this morning."

"Where did she go?"

"Far away! Out of the country to the missions and I'll never see her again!"

"I'm sorry, Gina! I'll leave you alone! I'll see you later, okay?"

Gina's mood was gloomy the entire morning. She missed Miss Alexis.

After lunch, Ellen joined Gina playing a game of checkers, but Gina could not concentrate. Her thoughts continuously reverted to Miss Alexis.

Suddenly, Janet came rushing into the dormitory panting excitedly. "Did you hear? Did you hear? Miss Alexis was killed in a plane crash!" Janet's words were crushing. Gina's little heart began to pound like crazy.

"Ah, that's a lot of bull." Joyce voiced.

"No, it's not bull! I just came from the office; a lot of teachers and nursemaids are there talking about it," Janet insisted.

"No! No!" Gina cried out. "It's not true! Oh, please, it can't be true!"

"Take it easy, Gina!" Ellen said. "Those girls may be up to their old tricks. If you really want to find out, let's go to the office. C'mon, I'll go with you."

Swiftly they raced down the stairway and ran to the main building. They sneaked into a dark room that was closest to the office and listened to the chatter.

"She was on her way to unite with the missionaries."

"Are they sure it was Miss Alexis who was killed?"

"Definitely. Everyone on the plane perished! It's a terrible shock. Miss Bower's, the new administrator, was notified a few hours ago."

"How tragic! Miss Alexis was a warm and loving person."

The words Gina had overheard cut through her like a knife. "I won't believe it! I don't believe it!

She cupped her hand over her mouth to smother her sobs.

In a daze, she left Ellen and took off running to the spare room. "Miss Alexis! Miss Alexis! She shouted repeatedly, rushing crazily around, flipping on the lights. "You didn't die, Miss Alexis! You didn't go away forever! You told me you would write me." Her tears flowed as she sat in Miss Alexis's chair wanting to die as well. "This is where we said goodbye, and now you're gone."

She wept hysterically and gazed towards the heavens. "Why? Why did you take her away? She was good and kind. I loved her." She argued with the Almighty, then stepping out of the chair she wobbled to the blackboard. She clumsily picked up a piece of chalk and wrote Miss Alexis, I love you.

She purposely screeched the chalk. "Remember! Remember, Miss Alexis," she called, imagining she were present. "You use to do that all the time and I would cringe, then we would giggle together."

221

She walked over to the jars of watercolors (which set on the counter) and opened several. "Remember, the first time we painted pictures; we were a mess." She stuck her finger into a jar, then another and another. "But you didn't care about the mess, and we would laugh about it."

She was in a stupor, and retraced her steps to sit on Miss Alexis's chair once more, gazing towards the heavens. "Why? Why do you take away what I love? I don't have anyone, any more! Everyone I need you take away from me. Why? I don't understand!" She rested her weary head on the desk, glaring at the gold cross dangling from her neck. She cried her heart out for her loving friend who would never return, eventually falling asleep.

"Gina!" She was awakened by Ellen's call. She raised her head, feeling dizzy, and felt Ellen's hand upon her shoulder. "Gina, it's not good for you to stay here in the spare room; when you left me last night, I followed you. I heard you crying and I thought best to leave you alone. I didn't see you in bed this morning so I figured I'd find you where I'd left you, and here I am," Ellen tried to jest.

"I'm sorry I left you, Ellen." Gina said sadly.

"It's okay," she smiled. "I understood. C'mon now, let's go to the bathroom and rinse those swollen eyes of yours. That's what my mother does to my brother when he cries a lot; I think your hands need washing too."

Ellen was a true and loyal friend. She understood Gina's agony and the anguish she bore. She was patient and didn't criticize her tears, yet, deep in Gina's heart, she feared to love her friend Ellen for she felt cursed because all that she tended to love eventually got taken from her and she was afraid of losing Ellen as well!

Gina felt dead within her very soul. She was on her feet, but walking in a fog. Miss Alexis was dead. Gone forever and she felt lost all over again. She feared growing up in the outside world with no one to love her. She hadn't gone to breakfast and chose just to lay in bed. Quietly weeping, she stared out the window, when she heard, "Gina!" In a flash she sat up thinking she'd heard Miss Alexis call.

"Miss Alexis! Miss Alexis, is it you?" She cried out peering through her tears.

"No, dear, it's Miss Tyler. I came to visit with you for a while. Ellen told me where I'd find you."

"Oh, Miss Tyler. Miss Tyler! My Miss Alexis is gone." Gina nestled in her arms, sobbing. "Why did she have to die? It just isn't fair! I loved her so much."

"Cry it out, dear! Cry it out!" She rocked her, comforting. "I can feel what you're going through, but you must snap out of it. You don't want to make yourself sick."

"It's hard for me to forget her! She was going to write to me. I was her little girl, she said." Gina sniffled.

"And she'd want her little girl to be strong; and you must be strong. You mustn't let her down."

"I've tried to be strong! Really! And in another day I'll be leaving here and I'll be all alone again. I don't know where Miss Jacobs will be taking me next!"

"Miss Jacobs. Who is Miss Jacobs?"

"You don't know her? She's scary! She's my social worker. She's the lady who brought me to this awful school!"

"Do you know anything about her?"

"No! She never talks or smiles!"

"Well, I think I'll look her up. Do you know where her office is?"

"It's an orphanage, someplace! I've been there a few times, but I don't know where it is! Oh, Miss Tyler, I'm scared. I miss Miss Alexis! Why did she have to die?" Gina cried.

"You know, dear, people don't die entirely. What I mean is, Miss Alexis is gone, but all her good qualities and teachings, she left behind in you."

"You mean like all the things she taught me?"

"Exactly dear! She instilled in you what she was taught in life; it goes on and on. Do you remember when you told myself and the counselors that Miss Alexis taught you always to tell the truth! Well, there's a good example; Truthfulness will be with you for a lifetime--which she handed down to you. So you see, dear, Miss Alexis may be gone, body and soul, but her teachings shall walk with you through life; a little of her is within yourself. She'll walk beside you spiritually."

"I think I understand; it's like she's still alive but through me. Then I'll be strong; she taught me that!"

"Now! Do you feel a little better, dear?"

"Yes, Miss Tyler, now that you told me what you did!"

"I'm glad, dear!" Miss Tyler stroked Gina's hair, fondly, "And now, I want to talk about the day when myself and the other counselors were questioning you. I had said something very crude--that you didn't exist--remember that?"

"Yes! I wondered what it meant. Miss Alexis explained to me a little about it."

"Well dear, that remark troubled me. You certainly do exist Gina, and I do apologize for not clarifying the statement; At the time, I couldn't, but I'm here to do that now. I wish to shed some light on the matter which revolves around Miss Adler and Miss Orr."

Miss Tyler summed up the truth alright, accounting that Miss Adler had planned her little scheme before Gina had ever set foot into that horrible school. Miss Adler saw a chance for financial gain by intentionally failing to register Gina at the main office; it being the case, no one would ever surmise that Gina existed; it enabled Miss Adler to feel free and pocket any money (forwarded directly to her) by an unknown individual which was intended for Gina's care. Gina didn't have parents for Miss Adler to be concerned about--so who would be the wiser? Miss Orr had been conned into the deal as well. She only said that--greed was the name of their game!

Because everyone begrudged Gina's presence in the school, it benefitted Miss Adler and Miss Orr favorably. They permitted the girls the upper hand and the run of the school. Diane took leadership and the rest became history. Miss Adler and Miss Orr were in the driver's seat, and those devilish girls supported them all the way. Miss Alexis was the only thorn in Miss Adler's craw.

When Ellen was injured, unbeknown to Miss Adler, her scheme was to crumble. She knew Gina hadn't caused the injury and she certainly didn't want any of her precious darlings involved. She acted her role superbly and banked on the girls to accuse Gina. She had caught the culprit. Gina would be punished and confined, and that should satisfy Ellen's parents; so she thought...

Miss Adler hadn't considered that Ellen's mother would contact the main office. She was beginning to squirm then. No doubt, the counselors found it necessary to check through Gina's files, but they came up fruitless; Gina was never registered therefore, she didn't exist; that is what Miss Tyler had hinted and not that Gina didn't exist otherwise.

The counselor's journey to Ellen's home resulted into a miracle for Gina; and Miss Adler's downfall.

"Well, dear! That's it in a nutshell," Miss Tyler said. "I couldn't deny you the truth! After all you've suffered I felt it was the decent thing to do. I only hope that you can forgive. I realize you'll never forget!

And now, dear, I must depart. You're a sweet and loving little girl; always stay that way; just for Miss Alexis."

"Thank you, Miss Tyler for visiting and telling me the truth. It was nice of you. You've helped me a lot. I won't cry so much and I'll be strong."

"Goodbye, Gina. Take good care."

"Goodbye, Miss Tyler."

Although Miss Tyler's words consoled and comforted Gina, she spent the remainder of the day weeping and remembering, dear Miss Alexis.

The following morning Gina was alone in the dormitory gathering her few belongings; preparing to leave the school, when she heard Ellen call. She turned and saw her holding in midair a blue suitcase.

"It's for you, Gina. My parents bought it for you," she handed it to Gina.

"They really bought it for me? Oh, it's so nice. It's big, too! Now I won't have to use paper bags,"

Gina said gratefully. "Oh, Ellen, thank you and please thank your parents, too. They have been so kind!"

"It's a going away present to a swell friend who's all heart."

"I'll miss you, Ellen. Thank you for all you've done for me," tears filled her eyes.

"Hey, don't start to cry! We'll see each other again! Look, Gina, I wrote my full name and address on this paper," she handed it to her. "Write to me and maybe someday you can visit us. Gina, do you know where you're going?"

"No!" Gina shook her head. "Miss Jacobs, the social worker decides that. She should be waiting for me in the office now. I'd better hurry and pack."

"Take good care of yourself, Gina. Goodbye." Ellen hugged her and tearfully ran off.

"Goodbye, Ellen!" Gina yelled. "Goodbye, my dear friend." Gina tearfully commenced to pack.

She sat on her bed for the last time and casting her eyes towards the window, she gazed at the sky. "Goodbye, sweet, Miss Alexis. I will always love and cherish you, and I'll always remember your teachings. I hope you're happy with the angels in heaven." She whimpered then quickly put on her warm coat, grabbed hold of her suitcase and slowly pranced towards the swinging doors.

When glancing around the dormitory for that one last look strangely, she began to tremble. She imagined hearing wicked voices. She began visualizing Diane and her dummy pals teasing and laughing at her. She depicted Miss Adler and Miss Orr lunging and lashing at her with their handy wooden rulers. "No! Oh, no! Don't hit me no more!" She was screaming, backing herself up against the swinging doors. The suddenness of the doors opening and her nearly falling out the other side revived her senses.

A bit stunned, she shook her head, took a deep breath, then ran off to the office. Upon arriving there, to Gina's surprise, she noticed Miss Jacobs and Miss Tyler exiting an office. "Miss Tyler! Hi, Miss Tyler!" Gina called happily running over to her. "I didn't know you would be here. Will you be taking me somewhere else instead of Miss Jacobs?"

"No dear! I'm sorry! Miss Tyler replied and Gina pouted looking disappointedly. "I was aware that Miss Jacobs would be picking you up today, and so, I thought to arrive here at the school early and meet with her. And now, I wish to chat with you a bit before you leave. Do you mind?"

"Oh, no, I'd like that!"

Miss Tyler excused herself from Miss Jacobs, leading Gina into a vacated office, seating themselves. "Gina what I plan to tell you, I learned from Miss Jacobs. I realize that what I am about to relate will be complicated and confusing for you to thoroughly understand, but, I will attempt to be brief and as explanatory as possible."

Gina listened attentively as Miss Tyler made known that when Gina's parents had deceased, it was her maternal grandmother who had Gina placed into an orphanage. Gina's grandmother wanted no part of her. (The reason for her grandmother's actions had not been disclosed). Because Gina had never been adopted, her grandmother had been contacted frequently by particular social workers from the orphanage imploring that she have a change of heart and agree to rear Gina as her own, but to no avail...

Years, later, when Miss Jacobs had appeared on the scene, a financial deal had been struck between Miss Jacobs and Gina's grandmother. The deal was for Miss Jacobs to enroll Gina into a boarding school (any boarding school) for as long a time as possible and, in turn, Miss Jacobs would be rewarded financially. It had been clearly stipulated that Gina's grandmother would foot the bill for Gina's tuition and care--no matter what the cost...Miss Jacobs, however, swears ignorance concerning Miss Adler pocketing the funds for Gina's care.

Gina's grandmother had set forth to rid of Gina permanently and because of Miss Jacobs greed had accomplished her wicked mission.

"My grandmother must have hated me real bad," Gina spoke tearfully. "Do you know where my grandmother is Miss Tyler?"

"No dear, that is something I know nothing about and Miss Jacobs refused to divulge her whereabouts. I am aware you hurt terribly however, I felt you should be enlightened of the truth for future references because, strangely, the past always has a way of creeping up unexpectedly and I know you would want to be prepared for the unexpected; and now dear you best be leaving. I pray that wherever you settle life will be good to you."

"Goodbye, Miss Tyler! Thank you for telling me what you did and for everything else you did for me. I'll never forget it." They hugged lovingly, going their separate ways.

As usual, Miss Jacobs readily snapped her fingers and Gina, self-acting, followed her to the car. Gina settled nervously in the seat and when Miss Jacobs seated herself into the car, Gina dared to ask,

"Miss Jacobs, where are you taking me?"

"To a foster home," she mumbled, "The people are elderly and have two grown-up sons, The family is considered satisfactorily qualified as foster parents although, I make no promises, good or bad."

As Miss Jacobs drove between the high, black iron gate, Gina uplifted herself to see through the rear window to take one final glance of her god awful hell hole and her bit of heaven. She then easily sat herself down and looking ahead thinking, she reaped with hope that her future will favor much love, trust, respect and serenity and perhaps heal her wounds.

CHAPTER THIRTEEN

Gina casually unbuttoned her coat and watched the scenery rush by her. She remained silent except for a nagging cough that would attack her at times. Her hands felt cold and clammy and she was feeling jittery. She guessed it was because she was going to meet her new foster parents. She wanted so much to belong somewhere, and in her thoughts, she hoped that her foster parents would like her and that it would be a happy home.

Interrupting her thoughts, were sharp snapping sounds. She curiously glanced about, spotting a trail of small, black stones bouncing behind the car. "It's only the cinders and gravel that is scattered on the road to prevent cars from skidding on the snow," Miss Jacobs assured. "Don't concern yourself about it."

Shortly, Miss Jacobs began to slow the car down. She veered toward a curb of a city block and parked in front of an enormous, tan brick house.

"That's a big house!" Gina said admiringly. "Will I be living here?"

"Yes, and I hope you manage to stay a while!" Miss Jacobs replied sarcastically. "You can let yourself out of the car."

Clutching her blue suitcase, she followed Miss Jacobs through an opened, silver painted gate. Snow blanketed the landscaping and the several trees surrounding the house stood snow covered and barren.

They climbed several wide cement stairs and entered through an arched doorway leading into a vast vestibule. The window caught Gina's eye as it differed from what she had ever seen. It was in black squares and, within the squares, it held colorful glass that appeared wrinkled.

Miss Jacobs began to fuss with her granny glasses as her jumbo eyeballs examined several small pieces of shiny metal that were embedded into the wall and had printing on them. Beneath the metal sat black buttons, which were also embedded into the wall. Gina watched Miss Jacobs press in one of the buttons and quickly rush over to a closed, clear glass, paned door. Within seconds, a loud buzzer sounded. Miss Jacobs pushed in on the doorknob and the door magically opened.

Thoroughly impressed, Gina said, "How did you do that, Miss Jacobs?"

"Oh, no matter," Miss Jacobs waved her hand annoyingly. "Just follow me."

They entered a smaller vestibule that was dimly lit and they stood in front of a solid closed door, in silence. Shortly, the door was opened wide, and a light turned on simultaneously. Standing in the doorway, pondering at them was a petite, elderly lady with olive, black eyes and graying short hair.

"Hello, Mrs. Ducci. I brought Gina Haskol."

"Ah, yes! Come'a in, please'a," Mrs. Ducci invited in a native accent. They followed Mrs. Ducci through a long foyer and about midway Gina noticed a glass-paned door which was closed. Several steps beyond, sat a solid brown colored door, which was also shut. Further ahead they entered a sizable, combination dining room and kitchen area.

"Sit down, please'a," Mrs. Ducci offered.

"Thank you, no! I must leave immediately," Miss Jacobs said.

"I'm in a great hurry. I'm sure Gina will be happy here and I'll be in touch with you regarding her physicals. Goodbye, Mrs. Ducci and thank you." She wiggled her skinny torso out the door.

Momentarily, Gina felt deserted, but Mrs. Ducci must have sensed her anxieties, and nearing her said, "No be'a scared! Im'a take'a care'a you! You pretty girl." She gently stroked her cheek. "You short like'a me'a, but you so skinny! Im'a get you fat," she giggled as she guided Gina into the kitchen. "How old you, Gina?"

"I'll be twelve come spring."

"Im'a like'a you hair! You keep nice'a." Suddenly, out of the blue, Gina visualized in her mind the horror of when her hair was cut forcefully; trying to block it out. "Gina, what you think about?"

"Oh, just something that happened at that terrible school! It's nothing!"

"I ask! You hungry?"

"I'm a little bit hungry." Gina was starving.

"Okay, Im'a make'a you sandwich. You like'a salami?"

"I've never eaten salami, but I'll learn to eat everything you serve."

"Va bene!"

"What did you say, Mrs. Ducci?"

"Oh Im'a forget! You no speak Italiano! I say very good. Im'a speak Italiano. We all Italiano in This house'a." She explained. "You learn to speak too." She prepared the salami sandwich and set it upon a child's table that sat beside the refrigerator. "You sit down an'a eat now." She poured a glass of milk.

Gina bit into the sandwich and found the salami mighty tasty, raving to Mrs. Ducci (with a full mouth) how delicious the sandwich was.

"Im'a know you like'a it. Everybody do! Let'a you help me cook the spaghetti an'a meat'aballs. Im'a teach you cook Italiano."

"I'd like that." Gina's tension was lessening.

"My son, Phillipo, he twenty-two an'a Carlo, he twenty-four, they like'a the spaghetti. You like'a spaghetti, Gina?"

"Yes, whenever I got to eat any of it." Gina suffered a slip of the tongue.

"What you mean?"

"Oh, it was at that crazy boarding school," Gina sighed. "This girl, Diane! Well, she looked like a big cow; she use to steal food all the time and gobble it like a pig! She was so mean and hateful. I hated her!"

"Quell Bastia!" Mrs. Ducci shouted. "Oh, Im'a forgot again," she grinned. "Im'a call that girl, beast."

"Everybody was so mean to me at that school; just because I was poor and an orphan and they were rich. They would hit me all the time. My mommy and daddy are dead, you know."

"Si, Si! Miss Jacobs, she tell me'a everything! You try an'a forget. You be happy here."

"Mrs. Ducci, where are your sons?"

"They go work. Im'a no know how long they keep work! They no know nothing! Im'a spoil them! All they want is eat an'a show off! They want to be big shot! It'a my fault!" Mrs. Ducci balked.

"Im'a wish they get married, but no girl like'a them! Im'a the only one'a work all the time'a. Today I take'a off. Im'aknow you come'a, but I stay home'a until you get use'a to everything an'a you go to school."

"Mrs. Ducci, what kind of work do you do?"

"Im'a sew lady braziers," she chuckled. "They hold you chest up," she placed both her hands under her breasts, bouncing them. "When you grow, you wear too!"

The slam of a door interrupted their conversation when a tall, robust, elderly man entered the dining room. He wore a stern, poker face expression, reminding Gina of Miss Adler from the boarding school. Mrs. Ducci quickly neared the man then turned to look back at Gina. "Gina," she called. "This Mr.Ducci, my husband." She looked back at him. "Paulo," she called him. "This Gina! She'a gonn'a live'a here'a."

Without a doubt, Gina sensed that Mr. Ducci was not impressed with her presence. He slowly walked over to a chair and sat himself down. The rays of the afternoon sun beaming through the window cast a sleek sheen atop of his balding head, and it appeared as if he had just finished shining it.

The silence seemed to irk Mrs. Ducci when suddenly, she began to spout at Mr. Ducci in Italian. Mr. Ducci retorted, also in Italian then they began shouting atop of one another's voice which seemed to infuriate the situation further. Their hands were waving in midair as rapidly as their mouths and neither of them seemed to be giving an inch.

Frightened, Gina stared at them. She sensed the argument related to her and it upset her. Eventually, the fiery feud subsided and Mrs. Ducci rushed over to Gina and said, "No you worry about Paulo. He'a get use'a to you. You call me'a Momma Ducci an'a Paulo, Poppa Ducci."

"Will it be okay with Mr. Ducci? I don't think he likes me!" Gina spoke in skepticism.

"Eh, me'a sure'a," Mrs. Ducci squealed, waving her hand at Mr. Ducci as if to let him know she wore the pants in the family.

Mr. Ducci lifted himself out of his chair and walked over to Gina. His squinty brown eyes glared down at her as he said, "You good girl, you stay! You make'a trouble, I'a punish you, an'a you go!"

Quickly, Mrs. Ducci intervened, yelling, "No, you no hit her. She'a get hit enough in that'a school she'a come from! You no do nothing. Comprendo!"

Mr. Ducci frowned defiantly at her and stomped out of the room in a huff. He disappeared behind the solid brown door Gina had observed earlier.

"He'a go down in the base'ament. It'a like'a apartment down there'a an'a Paulo, he'a like'a be alone'a"

"I'm sorry I caused trouble, Mrs. Ducci."

"No you worry. An'a you call me'a Momma Ducci, ricordo! I forget! Ricordo, it mean remember. My English no so good."

"I'll remember, Momma Ducci."

This quick transformation from the boarding school to Momma Ducci's home was like night and day. In just a short time, Gina felt somewhat comfortable. Momma Ducci made her feel that way; and for Gina to address an individual Momma thrilled her within.

"An'a now, I show you the room you sleep." Gina picked up her suitcase and followed Momma Ducci through a hallway. The bathroom was tiled in pale blue with black trimming. Adjacent to the bathroom was a spacious bedroom that looked like a studio room Gina had seen in magazines. "This Phillipo room," Momma Ducci pointed as they walked further sighting another bedroom that was untidy. "This Carlo room! He'a so sloppy an'a lazy." They veered a corner passing another bedroom. "That room Im'a sleep," she paused. "An'a Paulo," she added as they neared the last room.

"This you room." Gina looked around overwhelmed. "You like'a?" Momma Ducci smiled.

"Oh, do I! It's beautiful! It's so big and pretty. The yellow bedspread and the curtains make the room so cheerful. Thank you, Momma Ducci. This is all so new for me. I can't believe this is all happening!"

"You put you clothes'a in the dresser. You use'a the closet too. Im'a go in the kitchen an'a start cook."

"I'll be quick so I can help," Gina assured, and not wasting any time began to unpack, carefully tucking away her most treasured possessions.

Before Gina left for the kitchen, she peered out the rear window and saw a spacious cemented yard. In the middle of the yard set a large pavilion. Within the pavilion set a long wooden table and benches on either side. Gina had outdone herself, she thought and truly felt she could be happy in her new surroundings. For a spell, she looked towards the sky imagining Miss Alexis smiling down upon her and fancied her voice, "Be happy, dear! You deserve it." and just as sudden, Miss Alexis disappeared.

When Gina returned to the kitchen two young men had entered the dining room. Their brown hair appeared windblown and their short, stout frames slouched slightly. They were by no means dashing, and their brown eyes cast a look of disgust.

"Hey, ma," one of the men called. "Who the hell is she?"

"Silenzio, Carlo," Momma Ducci reprimanded. "This Gina. She'a gonn'a live'a here'a"

"No shit!"

"Shutt'a y'a mouth, Carlo! Im'a no want to hear you. Comprendo!"

"Ma, you're getting too old for kids," the other man spoke. "When the hell will you give up? We don't need no brats floating around."

"When Im'a dead! An'a you shutt'a y'a mouth too, Phillipo."
Momma Ducci busied herself with her cooking and the men left the
room smirking. "Those'a boys! They show no respect." She slid the
spaghetti into a huge pot of boiling water and stirred. Gina helped
set the table as best she could when Momma Ducci walked over to
the basement door and shouted, "Paulo, veni a mangi!" And in the
same breath called to her sons.

Supper was served and all three men greedily ate their food as if
they hadn't eaten in days. Conversation was nil until Carlo piped up
and said, "Hey, pop! What the hell do you think of this ugly puss of
a kid that's going to live here?"

"Brutto faccia you, Carlo! Gina, she pretty girl! She'a no ugly!
An'a Im'a no want to hear you say no more'a! Capish? Understand
Carlo?" Momma Ducci lashed out vehemently.

Poppa Ducci was quick to say, "Im'a no say nothing! She'a be
good, she'a stay! An'a that's all!" The conversation ended.

When supper was through, all three men rudely left the table without excusing themselves or conveying a word of gratitude to Momma Ducci. Gina thought them ungrateful cads and that they didn't know how lucky they were to be fed so generously and tended to so well.

Gina graciously praised Momma Ducci for a delicious supper; helped with the chores and by nightfall, she was exhausted.

"Gina," Momma Ducci called. "You go sleep when you want."

"I think I'll go now! Thank you for everything, Momma Ducci. You've made me feel so welcome. I haven't felt like that in so long. Goodnight!" she scooted off.

CHAPTER FOURTEEN

Ten years of Gina's young life, she would chalk up to a horrible experience. However, in a month's time, she had adjusted nicely in her new home. She was finally content and at peace with herself.

Momma Ducci was most attentive to Gina and showed interest in her well-being, but rarely did she display affection toward her. Gina picked up Momma Ducci's cooking tactics easily. She was happy that Momma Ducci trusted her to cook and bake. The household chores came easily for Gina as she had plenty of practice when she was in the boarding school.

Poppa Ducci would converse with Gina, but only when necessary. "You wash'a the dish'a! You shovel the snow! You scrub'a the marble'a staircase'a an'a mopp'a the vestibule hall too!

You clean the base'ament, domani! That'a mean'a tomorrow." He would correct himself. He commanded and Gina obeyed.

Poppa Ducci consistently wore black and white striped overalls and a long sleeved shirt or sweater. Come Sundays, he dressed in street wear attire as did both his sons. Poppa Ducci was an enthusiast in maintenance of the house; his sons showed no interest in that area.

Gina found it strange that whenever she was in the vast guest room and parlor, vacuuming the rug or polishing the old-fashioned furniture, Poppa Ducci would enter the room. He would make himself comfortable sitting on a chair or on a sofa chair, and watch her work. His presence made her awfully uncomfortable especially when she would catch Poppa Ducci casting insidious glances at her or making odd facial gestures. At times, when she would near him while dusting, he would easily feel under her dress, patting her butt and rub her thighs. Gina couldn't understand his behavior, and thought him weird as she would hastily leave the room.

Phillipo and Carlo were of the same temperament as Poppa Ducci--cocky with words. They relished giving orders and expected Gina to bow to their every demand. "I ain't got a fork! Get it, Gina! I want more sauce! Get me some, Gina! Clean my room, Gina!" Do this, Gina and do that, Gina! They all grunted out their demands. She thought authority had gone to their heads. Gina was kept hopping, but never objected. She was away from that horrible school and that's all that mattered to her.

Momma Ducci had enrolled Gina into a public grade school. It was a wonderful feeling for Gina to be accepted in class as just another ordinary kid, other than an orphan. The school was approximately a half mile distance from the Ducci home but Gina didn't mind walking. She enjoyed stopping at the different stores to look at the attractive window displays, particularly the toy and gift shops.

The school structure was similar to that of the boarding school consisting of steel, silver painted, staircases and long hallways. The pupil's desks and seats were individually bolted to the floor, and each had its own inkwell. The windows were high, and a long pole was used to open and shut them. Every morning, the "Pledge of Allegiance" was recited, then class would commence.

Gina was a good student and did fairly well in all her grades. English grammar and mathematics were her most difficult; as was in boarding school. Spelling and social studies had always been her favorite subjects. She had developed a special talent for art, and always felt so proud when one of her drawings was hung on the wall in the outer hallway of the classroom. It gave her a sense of accomplishment.

The diversion for the students, during class, was playing the game called "Simple-Simon." The teacher would stand in front of the classroom and voice to the pupils, "Simple-Simon say's, wiggle your nose." and the pupils would do so. When the teacher omitted the word "say's," and used another word in its place, the pupils remained in their rightful positions. If a pupil did otherwise, he or she was eliminated from the game until the last pupil was left standing and became the winner of that round; a lollipop went to the winner, then a new game resumed. At times, the teacher would recite so quickly that it was a wonder she didn't get tongue-tied. Gina couldn't help but get confused into doing one thing rather than another. The teacher enjoyed the humor, and laughed in accordance.

The game always created a cheerful atmosphere, like the time a pupil name Ralph, the chubbiest boy in the class, found himself in an awkward situation. The pupils were all stooped over, trying to touch their toes, when Gina heard something ripping. Slowly, she lifted her head and, to her surprise, noticed Ralph had split the back seat of his trousers wide open, and his butt was staring her right in her face. (Ralph wasn't wearing any underwear). Gina gasped and locked her lips together, trying to restrain from laughing. Some of the other pupils were quick to notice, and together they pointed, giggling crazily. Poor Ralph, he quickly stood upright, holding the seat of his pants together while the puffy cheeks of his face turned a rosy red. He waddled out of the classroom then, all the children exploded in laughter. School was fun for Gina and she never missed a day. Her friends were numerous and she was in seventh heaven!

Months quickly drifted and spring popped out all over. Momma Ducci surprised Gina with a birthday cake and had invited Gina's two neighbor girlfriends, Sharon and Linda, to help celebrate. Sharon was the same age as Gina, and always jovial, and when she laughed her blue eyes sparkled. She constantly brought to mind Gina's dear friend Ellen from the boarding school. Linda was blessed with a nasty disposition and was a year older than both girls. Often, Linda would become belligerent and she would angrily take hold of one Gina's long brown braids, stick it in to her mouth then wrench her blue eyes to get a point across. Sharon tolerated Linda's tantrums, but when she'd had enough, She'd chase Linda off to play by her lonesome.

Momma Ducci had gifted Gina with a pair of steel roller skates and permitted her to use them that very day. Gina couldn't explain the happiness she felt. Sharon and Gina walked a block away from the house and skated on the asphalt pavement. Sharon helped Gina coordinate her balance and form until Gina learned to stay on her feet rather than taking flops and nose dives.

Most every day, after school, when Gina completed her homework and chores, she would skate with Sharon. Sometimes, Poppa Ducci would detain Gina giving her extra chores to do. Gina didn't particularly enjoy it, but she accommodated.

One day, Poppa Ducci ordered her to scrub down the stairs leading to the basement. With the bucket of water at her side, and in a kneeling position, exposing her panties and legs, she scrubbed vigorously. She wanted to get the job done to go out skating with Sharon. She hadn't heard Poppa Ducci sneak up behind her when suddenly, she felt her rear being patted and diddling between her legs. She panicked hearing Poppa Ducci utter words in Italian she didn't understand. In an effort to avoid him, she accidently pushed over the bucket of water and it tumbled down the stairs. Poppa Ducci made a quick exit and Gina was in a dither trying to mop up the water and at the same time racking her brain wondering why Poppa Ducci had violated her in that manner. She didn't know what to think. She could only convince herself that perhaps Poppa Ducci's strange behavior was merely a display of approval for her labor. She was much too naive and content to suspect evilness.

Gina saddened when it came nearing the end of the month of June. Schools were closing for the summer vacation. She'd miss her friends and good times.

The Fourth of July, was celebrated with guests and a cookout in the backyard under the pavilion. It was Gina's dream come true. She finally felt that she belonged somewhere and she felt exuberantly joyous. By nightfall, firecrackers and sparklers concluded the festivities.

During each day that passed, many of the kids in the neighborhood, along with Gina, joined together playing punch ball, hide-and-seek, hop scotch and many other games. Other days, some of the kids would tag along with Gina to catch butterflies that she would press and place on cotton inside a glass frame.

Gina enjoyed putting picture puzzles together. She'd glue the pieces together and place it under the clear, long, plate glass that covered the top of the old-fashioned buffet. Momma Ducci called it a sideboard. Cut-out dolls and playing the old-fashioned player piano were other pastimes.

Two weeks before Labor Day, Momma Ducci took leave of absence from her job to prepare for canning fruits and vegetables. She and Gina labored from early morning to late evening in the basement peeling, mashing, straining, cooking and finally jarring. For Gina it was a tedious job, but it was most learned.

Poppa Ducci busied himself with the pruning of trees and landscaping the many assortment of flowers and bushes in the garden. Phillipo and Carlo were unemployed for the third time and made themselves scarce around the house. They were to say the least, allergic to work.

It troubled Gina that Momma Ducci didn't have control over her son's way of life, and Poppa Ducci cared less. However, Momma Ducci constantly harped at Gina, "You keep'a you leg close'a when yousit! You cove'a you knee'a with you dress! You no bend down so you coolie no show!" She would never explain her words of advice, but Gina did concern herself wondering about Poppa Ducci's unwelcomed familiarity upon her body!

In several days, school would be reopening and Gina was very anxious to return. Phillipo and Carlo were supposedly seeking jobs, and Poppa Ducci, Gina had learned was retired from work due to an industrial injury. Momma Ducci had returned to work and the days rolled on routinely.

It was one of those rainy, September afternoons, when Gina was returning home from school. She was drenched to the bone. She dashed to her bedroom. She gathered dry clothing then raced to the bathroom, closing the door behind her. When dressed, nature called.

She sat on the commode when suddenly she eyed the doorknob turning and the door opening. Gina sank back alarmed and hollered, "Poppa Ducci, I'm in here. I'll be finished soon." It was as if he never heard her words. He took a few steps inward and shut the door behind him. He walked over to the washstand that was adjacent to the bowl and halted. Gina became distressed. She didn't know what to pay attention to, letting herself out or Poppa Ducci. She only knew he didn't belong!

She reached for the doorknob when Poppa Ducci grabbed her wrist, stopping her dead in her tracks. "You stay here'a with me'a," he growled insisting he was going to show her something nice.

"No!" Gina shouted. "You don't belong in here. I want to go! I don't want to see anything!" Yet she didn't really know what she didn't want to see; It was only her natural girlish instincts reacting, and she was anxious to flee.

"You stay!" He squeezed tighter on her wrist and reaching with his other hand, snatched off her panties. She sobbed bitterly as he backed up, pulling her with him, and sat on the edge of the bathtub. Desperately, she pulled and tugged to free herself when he reached under her dress and began fondling her down there. "Io piacere giocare! Im'a like'a play with you!" He'd muttered those same Italian words during the basement incident.

She was out of her mind with fear watching him rise to his feet and unbutton the lower front of his overalls. She had no idea what he intended. She threatened to tell Momma Ducci. He flared at her, shaking her violently and warned her that if she spoke one word he would send her to a worse place than where she came from

She was torn. She didn't want to be sent away. She was happy in this home and vowed over and over again, she wouldn't tell. On that note, Poppa Ducci exposed himself. Gina's tearful eyes widened like marbles shocked at the ugly spectacle before her; For she had never seen the lower extremities of the male species.

Poppa Ducci pulled her towards the commode, pushing her on to it, and she struggled free. He angered at her persistent wailing, slapped her face, then lifted her bodily back on to the commode. She was trembling fiercely when he turned on the water spigot. He picked up the bar of soap and began lathering his extremity. He reached for Gina's hand. She pulled away, but he managed to grab one of them and forced it closed around that thing. She continued pleading to release her when he began to stroke himself in abrupt motions. She felt the thing swell and stretched her fingers to avoid it. He almost broke her fingers clasping them beneath his hand as he jerked with more urgency, yanking her off the bowl. She turned her head away ashamed of the sordid ordeal, when she heard panting.

He paused momentarily, rinsed her hand, then released her. She begged to leave when Poppa Ducci reminded her of his threat. She promised and frantically ran to her room.

She was beginning to understand that Poppa Ducci's roaming hands, insidious glances and hideous, facial gestures towards her, meant more than him being a weirdo; as she thought him to be. It was all leading up to this unsuspecting repulsive moment. She was pitiful. Her contentment had been limited to a few short months, as within minutes, Poppa Ducci had turned her world around.

From that day, Gina's life became a pretext, a mockery, and she knew she would live in fear, but not understanding the vile act Poppa Ducci committed. No matter how she tried, she couldn't erase the ugly episode out of her mind, nor could she ever erase the scorn she held for him.

In school, she professed to be content, and in the Ducci home, Poppa Ducci's piercing eyes were a constant reminder to keep her mouth shut! And she did for fear of horrible punishment.

Late in October, Momma Ducci and Gina were journeying to a particular destination. "It for you physical," Momma Ducci expressed and Gina was leery. She believed it to be a hoax, and that Poppa Ducci was having her sent away to some awful place; she thought he was fearful that she might reveal the truth about him.

As they arrived, Gina recognized the building immediately, announcing that she knew the place and was here lots of times when she was younger. She'd mentioned, she use to call it her, "Old stomping grounds."

They entered the building, registered, and Gina was given a white hospital gown to change into. They sat in an enormous waiting room which consisted of long, black benches with back rests aligned in succession. Kids, young and old were everywhere, and all were orphans registered for physicals. Out of the blue, Gina voiced, "Momma Ducci! After my physical, is Miss Jacobs going to take me someplace else?"

"No! You no go nowhere'a except with me'a," she assured, and Gina felt relieved.

It was a long time waiting, when Gina heard her name called, and alone, she entered the examination room. Awaiting her, was a male doctor. He appeared to be a gentle sort; however, it didn't alter Gina's intense distrust regarding men. "You won't hurt me," she sputtered nervously, wanting to run.

He assured her and she shied over to him holding her gown closed behind her. The doctor handled her with tender care, and thoroughly satisfied with her health status, discharged her.

A special Thanksgiving Day dinner was being served at the Ducci home, and Gina's nostrils filled with delicious aromas of food. Momma Ducci had prepared much of the food the evening prior; it allowed her time to spend with the guests, she'd mentioned.

On this memorable day, Gina planned to set aside her fears and enjoy the day. She prepared (on a large oval platter) the appetizer; called in Italian "Antipasto" made up of a variety of Italian cheeses, cold cuts and rare delicacies.

The guests had arrived and everyone gathered into the spacious dining room and sat themselves at the long, rectangular table, of which Gina had set the plates, cutlery, glasses and accessories upon, earlier. The guests accepted Gina warmly and complimented her on the beautiful table setting and the antipasto which sat in the center of the table. The guests were all Italian kin folk. They spoke Italian fluently, and English they spoke with a native accent.

A prayer was versed and it was time to indulge! Momma Ducci carried in the turkey and the guests carried on like kids. Gina was remembering boarding school and the torment she'd suffered. She was so grateful for this day!

Red and white wine flowed; even Gina was offered a glass. She loved it, asking for more! The more food brought in, the more was devoured; like the old saying, "From soup to nuts." The guests had brought with them Italian pastries and cookies; something Gina never had before. "Oh, they were delicious." The meal seemed endless and was topped off with everyone sipping liqueur; a green colored liquor with aromatic substances. Gina, smacked her lips, like a cat lapping milk. Come nightfall, the guests departed. The chores were completed and Gina retired to bed, stuffed to the gills, and oh, so happy.

In the morning, Gina awakened, stretching and yawning, and still stuffed from the Thanksgiving dinner. She washed and dressed then headed for the kitchen. She noticed no one was present. It wasn't unusual that she remained alone in the house, but it always gave her a scary feeling; especially being alone with Poppa Ducci. He'd given her cause for fear.

She was bogged down with extra school assignments due to the holiday, and thought it best to challenge them. She sat at the dining room table, concentrating, when shortly, Poppa Ducci entered the room. She became tense and her heart thumped faster. She was remembering that horrible day and was scared stiff.

"E' carino, you leave'a you work! You come'a with me'a!" He said.

Gina calmly explained that she had lots of homework and didn't want to go anywhere with him.

He heated at her words that were persisting she go with him. "Io volla giocare," He yanked her out of the chair.

She implored him to leave her alone, and trying to alarm him, mentioned that his sons would be returning and they would tell Momma Ducci.

He shrugged off the remark squabbling that his sons were smart boys and they wouldn't say a word. He then, forcefully dragged Gina into her bedroom, shutting the door behind them. "Im'a want'a play, an'a you gonn'a be'a good girl."

She was screaming, begging him to let her go, but her plea's fell upon deaf ears. Poppa Ducci viciously flung her on the bed. She kicked and struggled and booted him in the chest. He angered. He pulled off her shoes and positioned her that her legs would dangle off the edge of the bed. He rested against them. She tried to push herself up, but it was useless. Crying frantically, she wondered what he was going to do to her. She was too innocent to understand this aspect of abuse. He pulled out a towel from inside the bib of his overalls, then she felt his heavy hands roughly pull off her undies. She burst into hysteria as he placed the towel under her rear.

"Silenzio," he demanded, whacking her repeatedly on her rump. Shocked, she opened her tear-filled eyes and saw him unfastening his overalls. Relentlessly, she wept in horror, seeing that thing again. He began to ravish her frail body as she felt him trying to wheedle his extremity into her being, coaxing forcibly. Screams of pain died in her throat, and she began beating on Poppa Ducci's arm which rested heavily across her chest. Suddenly, she felt agonizing penetration. She shrilled out of her mind, and felt to pass out; and, if ever one would want to die, she wanted to die then. Excruciating pain and tears prolonged as he relaxed. She faintly heard him threaten her once more to keep her mouth shut--or else! Uncaringly, he left fastening his overalls.

Gina's mind was shattered and her being, in agonizing pain as she lay weeping in stains of blood; was it any wonder that her thoughts would revert to Miss Alexis, remembering all her bountiful teachings, and they seemed shattered as well. She recalled all the horrible punishment she had yielded to in theboarding school; and those horrible occurrences reflected most strongly upon Poppa Ducci's threats even more so. Slowly, she maneuvered her limp body off the bed. She wiped herself dry with the towel, then threw it behind some boxes in the closet. She laid back on the bed, beneath the covers, dishonored for life!

Gina was much too young to apprehend the urgency of Poppa Ducci's crazed behavior. She dreadedthe loathsome game he played, and fought like a wildcat, as countless times thereafter, he maliciously raped her. Other times, he was like a mad man and forced her into performing other indecent acts. Her moral beliefs and emotional status had been so terrorized and she, experiencing bitter misery before, swore to adverse secrecy. Poppa Ducci reduced her to ruins, disgraced her for life and each day that followed, she lived a living hell!

The Christmas Holiday was a farce for Gina no matter how wonderful the holiday will be. She felt so alone and her heart was burdened with a grave secret. When Momma and Poppa Ducci presented her with wonderful Christmas gifts Gina couldn't understand how Poppa Ducci could be so cheerful and without conscience.

The ringing bells from the steeple of a church nearby, rang in the New Year as well as the miserable years which followed...and, there was no end to Poppa Ducci's immoral deeds - a child rapist.

CHAPTER FIFTEEN

At fourteen, Gina remained slim, sprouted in height and her chest was scantily endowed. In school, the boys forever taunted, and nicknamed her, "Spare Ribs and Fried Eggs." In the girls gym, locker room, they would tease, "Give them some pep talk, Gina! As the old saying goes, "What God has forgotten.Stuff with cotton." and Gina's face would blush.

Gina was flourishing into a young lady as her menstrual cycle appeared. She hadn't any knowledge of this unexpected occurrence.

Momma Ducci never prepared her for its appearance; and Gina truly believed she had cut herself, somehow, or Poppa Ducci had severely injured her. Two days, she wore washcloths to absorb the flow. She was distraught until she gathered courage and confronted Momma Ducci with the problem. She wasn't the least bit excited. "Most all girls get it! It normal! No you worry!" She explained retrieving a box from the bathroom cabinet. "You use'a down there'a! It finish soon!" She instructed, ending the matter. Gina had many questions to ask Momma Ducci, and lots of other questions regarding sex; but Momma Ducci got on her high-horse and refused to discuss anything.

Gina was older now, and had picked up bits and pieces about sex from the kids in school; yet, not clearly enough to understand Poppa Ducci's malign acts upon her. She couldn't figure Momma Ducci out. She was always cautious about Gina, yet, she refused to enlighten her about sex. In her mind, sex was "taboo." Gina was so confused and always left in the dark.

Phillipo and Carlo's lifestyle remained unveiling. However, their new, unsuspected advances towards Gina were appalling to her. A playful pat on her rear; a hand rubbing her legs, under the table; and the stroking of her long brown hair riled her and she would insist they keep their paws to themselves.

Momma Ducci would appear annoyed with Gina's snobbery, but seemed to enjoy the eagerness of her sons, doling their endearing young charms. "Im'a like'a my boys joke'a with you, Gina! You grow up'a now an'a my boys show you some things!" She hit a nerve, and Gina wondered about her wacky indifferences.

Gina detested all three men, and overhearing their many crude conversations, no doubt, Poppa Ducci confided sexually molesting her. "C'mon pop, you robbed the cradle; we want a chance to ball with her too! Dames don't dig us! Give us a break, pop!" They'd rattle on and on, and poor Gina would churn with fear.

On occasions, Gina would question Momma Ducci about her biology lessons. She would fly off the handle cussing out the teachers for instructing the subject. She didn't believe it should be taught in school and Gina wondered why she was so down on sex. Was that the reason she was so strict with Gina? She worked all day, didn't she think something could happen in her own home? One day, Gina cornered Momma Ducci and asked her those very questions. She was digging for answers and practically painted her a picture.

Momma Ducci got all shook up and on the offensive, defending her need to work and that she had no control over her family. "Whatever happen, Im'a no know! An'a Im'a no want to know! Capish? Conversation, finite!" She screeched. In other words, she was telling Gina that she didn't give a damn!

For some strange reason, Gina felt that Momma Ducci was avoiding the situation. Her enthusiastic reactions towards her son's attentiveness towards Gina, made it appear sensible to her, but what was Gina to do? There was no one to confide in and who would believe her?

Gina's neighbor girlfriends Sharon and Linda, had moved to another state, and she truly missed them. In school, she had become withdrawn and a loner. She was considered a bore, except to Mary who had befriended her, and never asked questions. Mary's sensitive nature, twinkling dark brown eyes, and dark black hair were an asset to her spunky spirit. She was so jovial the day she came running over to Gina as she was exiting the school building. "Gina! Gina!" She called excitedly. "How about you coming over to my house today? My mom said its okay."

"I'd love to, Mary, but I can't."

"Oh, c'mon, Gina! You can't live in a shell all your life."

"If Mrs. Ducci were to find out that I visited a friend's home without her," Gina paused. "She'd kill me."

"Just a little while. Please, Gina!"

"I really can't! Mrs. Ducci won't like it. She's so darn strict."

"What's the harm in visiting with a girlfriend? So-long as your family knows where you're at. Do you want me to ask your mom?"

"She's at work."

"So then, what's there to worry about?"

"Mr. Ducci is at home, and he'll hit me if I visited. I'm not allowed to do anything."

"I'm sorry, Gina! Really I am! "By the way my birthday is coming up." She told Gina the date and Gina excitedly responded that it was her birthday as well. "I want you to come to my party!" Mary said meaningfully. "And Gina, I don't mean to be nosey, but why do you call your mom and dad, Mr. and Mrs.?"

The question floored Gina, as she quickly searched her thoughts. No one knew she was an orphan, or a foster child, and she was not about to reveal the truth. "Oh, since I was a little kid. It's the way they taught me to address them. I really don't know exactly why, except that they're elderly, and I guess it gives them a sense of respect. They're real old fashion in their ways, but at home I call them Momma and Poppa Ducci." Gina hoped that Mary would accept her fictitious tale.

"Oh, okay!" Mary replied with a puzzled expression on her pretty face. "Well, anyway! It's notimportant. Cripes, Gina! You mean you'll never get to visit with me?"

"I doubt it, Mary! You shouldn't even bother with me anymore. I'm no good!"

"Don't say that, Gina! You're a good person! I'm not giving up on you either." Mary lifted Gina's spirits. "I like you a lot, Gina, no matter what the other kids think; and I understand." Mary was sincere, but Gina knew she didn't truly understand the hell, the pain, and mental havoc she endures. "So long, Gina, see you tomorrow."

"Bye, Mary! Thanks for inviting me." Gina began to venture home and began to think how much she resented Momma Ducci's strictness, and she felt that Momma Ducci should be combing the inside of her own home, rather than worrying about the outside world.

Columbus Day, was gray and dreary outdoors. School was out and, although a national holiday, Momma Ducci was at work. Gina had busied herself with household chores, cleaning the kitchencabinets. She thought it strange that Phillipo and Carlo were loafing around the house as they usually made themselves scarce. She was remembering their lewd conversations and became leery and uneasy. Poppa Ducci was sitting at the dining room table reading the Italian newspaper, when he rose out of his chair and calmly walked over to her, "Io volla giocare." He'd spoken his favorite expression.

Gina stood upright and boldly lashed out for him to "get lost and leave her alone." She mentioned how much she despised him and all the horrible things he'd done to her and forced her to do; then claimed that Momma Ducci plays dumb. She began to tremble and her eyes moistened mentioning that if only there were a person whom she could talk with and tell them about the abuse she had succumbed, she would. She didn't care anymore and in her frustration, she quickly thought to herself, who would believe her? No one dares mention the word sex. It's an evil word.

"You shut you mouth! You say nothing! Comprendo! He struck her across the face and in the same act voiced, "E' Phillipo, Carlo, vieni qui, subito."

Within seconds, they appeared with all smiles then all three forcefully dragged her into Phillipo's bedroom, slamming the door behind them. Gina fought, bit and scratched, but three against one was no match. They wrestled like a throng of wild beasts, disrobing her then each took his turn undressing themselves. She cried and begged pathetically to let her go, but her sobbing pleas did not soften their callous hearts. They were like animals with their tongues hanging out, when they roughly flung her on the sofa bed. Weeping hysterically, she embraced herself in shame as those merciless cads began to exploit her body.

She closed her tear-filled eyes as she couldn't bare the ugly nakedness before her. She heard them whimper and giggle unidentifiable words as their icy fingers and heavy hands coddled her everywhere. Grunting, struggling and straining helplessly to free herself, it happened. They each ruthlessly raped her repeatedly then gloated pleasurably.

From that dreadful day, for Gina, life became insignificant like the fowl scum on stagnant water. Everyday which passed, she lived unforgettable nightmares when each of the men exercised their crazed lust upon her; and is forced to endure their repulsive depravities. Sheer hate has devoured her soul; the scars shall remain within her eternally, and neither the men or Momma Ducci could

give a damn.

CHAPTER SIXTEEN

Two unmemorable years have passed and heaven only knows how Gina maintained her sanity. It was her sixteenth birthday. She was scheduled to meet with Miss Gross, the director of the orphanage where Gina had been placed at infancy. It was Miss Gross's duty to enlighten Gina regarding her heritage; a regularity that takes affect only when an orphaned child was never adopted.

Before arriving to the office, Momma Ducci walked over to the waiting room. Gina stepped into the office when Miss Gross invited her to sit in a green sofa chair waiting in silence for Miss Gross to speak. Miss Gross appropriated tact and finesse as she made known to Gina, that she was an illegitimate child. The shattering truth was a pounding blow to Gina's ego, but most of all, she felt ashamed of her birth right and refused to believe that she was a bastard child.

Tears streamed from her eyes and strangely, she recalled an incident from boarding school when Joyce, a student, had defined the word bastard to her friends mentioning, "It's really bad." and Gina wept more so. Miss Gross acknowledged further, "Your real mother is alive. Her name is Rita Haskol. I have no knowledge of her marital status! Regarding your real father, he is unknown!"

Gina struggled with the mounted pressure and, explosively, she lurched to her feet squealing, "My real mother is alive? She's really alive? Why wasn't I ever told? Why was it kept a secret? Why was I lied to all these years? Why! Why! Why!" She cried hysterically and wearily threw herself into her chairthinking of the hell she lived and, of which the truth may have prevented. Momentarily, Gina resented everyone who had robbed her of her mother's love; even more so, towards Momma Ducci. When Gina simmered, she asked Miss Gross dozens of questions. She desperately wanted to see and be with her mother.

Miss Gross squirmed slightly in her chair then calmly voiced that she was not at liberty to reveal any information of her mother's whereabouts. Gina sat dazed and could not rationalize Miss Gross's reasoning. "On this paper," Miss Gross said. "I have written your grandparent's name and telephone number." She handed Gina the paper. "Make use of it, and perhaps you may learn where your mother is." Hence, Gina vowed to find her real mother. "I wish you the best, Gina. I'm only sorry that I cannot inform you further. I'm bound to uphold regulations."

Gina's first attempt to phone her grandmother was a total disaster. The mere mention of Gina's name and who she was created havoc. Her grandmother fussed and fumed. She was evasive and refused to disclose any information or the whereabouts of Gina's mother. Gina failed to interpret her grandmother's hostility and was deeply disturbed. However, she had no intentions of giving up.

Other conversations took place that also resulted fruitless. However, during a particular conversation, Gina heard a strange woman's voice chime in. "This is your Aunt Lea and I dislike admitting it," she said nastily. "You're a menace and unwanted in our family! Just leave us the hell alone! We don't want a family scandal!"

Gina's ears scorched, when she heard her grandmother screeching, "You're a bastard! We don't want a bastard in our family!" Stabbing Gina with a knife would have been less painful. "Nobody knows you exist, and it will be over my dead body before you ever see your mother!"

"I don't understand! I'm your flesh and blood!" Gina cried.

"Like hell!" grandma flared. "I had your mother give you up, and I don't regret it! And, I stopped her from visiting you at those foster homes when you were little too, and now you know!" She slammed the receiver down.

Shocked, humiliated, and feeling miserable, Gina's thoughts recalled her special lady friend, Annie. She came to realize it was her real mother; and that her mother did care about her. That fact alone gave Gina the courage to continue her search. She loved her mother no matter what!

Gina collected herself as the heated words of her grandmother's voice burned in her mind. She damned her grandmother's masquerade, realizing that her illegitimacy would walk with her through life, and it is the price she'd pay for immorality and deceit.

Months drifted by, and much to Gina's disappointment, the phone conversations with her grandma ceased when she had disconnected her phone. It was unexpected and thenceforth, all Gina had going forher was her last name and unfaltering determination.

In the course of Gina's shameful and sordid life, she had already become a senior in high school. She involved herself in athletics; her favorite being running and swimming. Practicing for heats after school hours pleased her. It gave her the opportunity to remain away from the Ducci home; away from those evil men. In her spare time, she had exerted much thought as to possible avenues she might pursue in her search for her mother, but endlessly wound up a blind alley. She bore anxieties, and felt she would never find her mother.

Gina felt proud as a peacock strutting down the aisle, in the auditorium, preparing to receive her graduation diploma. It was one of a few happy times in her life. On her mind, was to attain a job and vanish from the Ducci home. Undoubtedly, Gina deeply resented Momma Ducci for denying her the valuable attention in times of need. Momma Ducci's old-fashioned upbringing and her damnation of sex had sealed her lips, closed her mind, shut her eyes, and allowed disgrace and suffering to descend upon Gina.

On the other hand, crazy as it may sound, Gina felt compassion for her; similar to Miss Adler from boarding school. Momma Ducci had worked so admirably for her family and received nothing in return; and she had instilled in Gina that simplicity in life was more valuable than all the luxuries we hope and dream for; and for this knowledge, Gina was grateful.

Job hunting wore the soles from under Gina's shoes, but in one month time, she had acquired a clerical position with a law firm. Her three years of commercial studies in school had benefitted her. She was tickled and within a few weeks, was free and out of the clutches of those three wicked men who had driven her to living hell.

Gina ventured to the big city. There she chose to reside in a rooming house for women. Sisters of a particular religious order served as attendants. They were all elderly, but young in heart and spirit. The women boarders were aged thirty five and over; Gina being the youngest. They were taken in by her youth and forever showed concern worrying about her wellbeing. Gina enjoyed the attention.

Time was shaping up in her life. There was no hell to contend with; and her fears and distrust were tapering. Her friends were few and, she hoped sincere.

Days passed by routinely on the job; typing, filing, the usual, until a young girl named Celia, about Gina's age, was hired. Celia had that mischievous look in her eyes and was hilariously goofy. She'd giggle at anything and everything. She always had Gina in stitches, laughing. They became real pals. They would spend their lunch breaks together strolling the city blocks. Celia was something else when she would pretend to be handicapped, holding out her hand for a donation. She'd get what she was after then cackle crazily. Gina would shake her head, smirking, thinking how crazy Celia was, but she was the best.

One day, Celia had bought a water gun. She stuck it into her pocket, allowing only the nozzle to peep through. As the two treaded along the tall buildings, Celia would suddenly squirt the water gun at someone. Instantly, that individual would immediately look upwards cussing out the pigeons, believing they had urinated on them. She'd get the biggest charge out of it, howling with her horse like laugh.

On another day, Celia had bought a water gun for Gina. She wanted to include her in the fun she had planned. "Today we'll go to the railroad station," Celia said excitedly. "We'll go on the balcony and squirt water on every man with a bald head. Are you game?"

Gina, being tamer of the two, smiled sheepishly, thinking the matter over, then said, "Oh heck! Okay, but I hope nothing comes of it."

And so, during lunch break, they set out to do their thing. Gina chickened out at first, but watching Celia squirting and going nuts, she joined in. Together, they were having a ball, giggling and joshing like kids, watching the bald headed men wipe their wet domes and looking puzzled. A while passed, when Celia had spotted three men walking side-by-side. The man in the center was bald headed as they come. "There's a beauty," Celia choked up, pointing, when just as quick, she aimed and squirted.

Unexpectedly, the girls saw the man point up towards them, then heard him voice, "'You up there! Stay where you are!" In dismay, they watched the men charge for the stairway and they froze as they neared them. "And what do you pistol packin' momma's think you're doing?" The bald headed man asked. Celia, for the first time was lost for words, and Gina was so scared, seemed to have lost her voice totally. "You two Annie Oakley's follow us." And so they did, into a small room located behind the train depots. The room was entirely wallpapered with photographs of wanted criminals. "See those mugs on the walls! That's where you gun slingers mugs ought to be." The man smirked a bit. "And by the way, I'm Detective O'Leary. These men are my associates; Also detectives." He rattled off their names. Both girls swallowed hard and wanted to crawl into a hole. Gutsy Celia loudly began stuttering apologies for both girls and that they meant no harm. "We were bored! Just having some fun! She concluded, giggling.

Lucky for the girls Detective O'Leary had a sense of humor. He had warned them both to keep out of trouble then released them. With a sigh of relief the girls departed.

A few days later, the girls took a notion and visited Detective O'Leary inviting him out to lunch as a peace offering. He happily accommodated and from that day on, they became a trio until his unexpected death. The girls attended his funeral and learned that the cause of death derived from an affliction called Pulmonary Tuberculosis which devastated both girls.

Three months later, Celia left her position to wed and reside overseas. Gina missed her immensely but also realized that life must go on. She continued working diligently on the job earning a promotion and, she would pursue life's challenges and persevere her eternal optimism and put her trust in faith, hope and charity with all her heart and soul.

THE END

www.ingramcontent.com/pod-product-compliance
Lightning Source LLC
Chambersburg PA
CBHW031111030726
47496CB00002BA/490